CANYON

OF

DEATH

The Jake Silver Adventure Series:

Saving Tom Black – Book I

Apache – Book II

Canyon of Death – Book III

CANYON OF DEATH

JERE D. JAMES

MOONLIGHT MESA
ASSOCIATES

CANYON OF DEATH

All Rights Reserved, ©2011 Moonlight Mesa Associates, Inc.

All rights reserved. No part of this book may be reproduced or transmitted in any form or by any means without the written permission of the publisher.

Printed in the United States of America

Published by:

Moonlight Mesa Associates, Inc.
18620 Moonlight Mesa Rd.
Wickenburg, AZ. 85390

www.moonlightmesaassociates.com
orders@moonlightmesaassociates.com

928-684-5235/5231

ISBN: 978-0-9827585-4-0

LCCN: 2011931603

To My Posse –

Tom, Jered, and Ben

Publisher's Note

Although this book is largely a work of fiction, we have included photos of the Chiricahua Mountains taken by the author during his six-month stay in the area while writing this novel. The Chiricahua Mountains were the last stronghold of the Apache people. The Chiricahua Apaches have a long, brutal, and bloody history regarding their effort to remain free. Many famous Apache leaders lived in or near this area: Cochise's stronghold is close by.

The area earned a rugged reputation during the last part of the nineteenth century. Cowboys, soldiers, miners, settlers, and Apaches all contributed to its roughness and violence. Towns such as Galeyville, Paradise, and Portal sprang up overnight, only to fade away because of the migration of miners heading for the next mother lode, and the danger and difficulty of homesteading. A few families did stay, and these persevering pioneers are excellently covered in R.W. Morrow's *The Chiricahua Journals*. But even those hardy souls were few in number.

Even now the Chiricahuas maintain a tarnished reputation due to the passage of illegal immigrants and drug smugglers throughout the area. The Canyon of Death referred to in this book is actually Rucker Canyon, home of the Arizona rancher recently murdered by an as yet unknown illegal Mexican assailant.

A geologic wonder, the Chiricahuas are part of the mountain chain often called "Sky Islands," a 70,000-square-mile area that stretches across the southwest from northern Mexico, to southwest New Mexico and across southeast Arizona. A section of the Chiricahuas has been designated a National Monument. Its splendor may not be as imposing as that of the Grand Canyon, but the monument's magnificence is every bit as impressive.

KAIBITO TRADING POST

"Been expecting you," Ben McGraw said as dust-covered, exhausted Marshal Jake Silver walked toward the Kaibito Trading Post.

Jake slowed, uncertain what that greeting meant. He studied McGraw, who was standing in the doorway of the stone building, seeing worry deeply etched in the burly man's face and eyes. Ben McGraw's whole posture indicated trouble.

An avalanche of possibilities cascaded through Jake's mind. He kept his eyes planted on McGraw, and sure enough, the man looked down, unable to bear his penetrating gaze.

Neither spoke for a moment as they stood, face to face. "What," Jake stated, more than asked.

"She's here. Indians brought her in yesterday."

Jake shoved past McGraw, forcing his way into the open room. "Where is she?"

"Jake, before you see her, I gotta warn you. She's not good." McGraw turned to follow Jake into the room.

"Where is she?" Jake demanded, louder.

"She's with Tilly. Shimasani's there, too." McGraw firmly grabbed Jake's arm. "Listen to me. Stop a damn minute and listen."

Despite his angst, Jake stood, waiting for the sinister news.

"She's not good. But there's hope. The doc from Freeman is on his way. Should be here tomorrow." McGraw paused before continuing. "I'm real sorry."

Jake stood a moment longer, his heart thumping. He hesitated before the heavy Navajo blanket that separated the sleeping quarters from the trading center, steeling himself. "What's happened to her, Ben?" he asked, stalling. "Help me out here."

CANYON OF DEATH

The large man gently placed his hand on Jake's shoulder. "She's been beat up pretty bad. The Indians found her in the desert. They kept her for a few days before bringing her here. Apparently, she was 'most dead when they found her. They didn't think she'd survive the trip here without some o' their care first." Pausing, McGraw cleared his throat. "They brought her in two days ago. She don't look too good, but she's holding her own as far as we can tell. Not gettin' worse, anyway. I'm real sorry to have to tell you this."

Jake took a long, deep breath, and entered the curtained room. A small window emitted enough light that he could see Betsy's bruised and battered face. Clumps of her long, blonde hair had been torn from her head. She looked so fragile, forlorn, and helpless lying in the middle of the bed. His breath jerked in, and he stifled a groan of anguish, instantly followed by a spasm of rage, then swiftly collapsing to a profound sense of grief and sorrow.

Tilly McGraw sat by Betsy's side holding vigil over the sleeping girl. On the other side of the bed, an older Indian woman, a Navajo called only Shimasani who lived with the local medicine man, mumbled incoherently in a sing-song voice, rocking slowly to and fro. Upon Jake's arrival Mrs. McGraw stood, motioning for him to take her place.

Sitting heavily, Jake felt the energy sucked from him. He held motionless for a moment, unable to tear his eyes from the floor to look Betsy full in the face. When finally he did so, he saw a swollen, blue eye watching him, the other eye, only a slit, unable to open. No smile. No tears. No sign of recognition crossed her face. Slowly, her eye closed, and her breath came in little puffs as she quivered slightly.

"Betsy," Jake whispered. "I'm here. I'm here. I'm never gonna leave you again." His throat constricted. *My god, what had he done? This was all his fault. No one's fault but his.*

He had no idea how long he sat, holding Betsy's small, delicate hand in his large, calloused one. At last, and for the first time in Jake's life, he prayed, bartering with God, pleading with Him, begging, finally demanding that He let her live.

Darkness fell, and suddenly he became aware of Tilly touching him lightly on the shoulder. "Jake, come eat something," she spoke softly.

"Shimasani will not leave her side. Come." Like a child, he arose and silently followed the slight woman, wanting only for someone to guide him at this moment through the helplessness and uselessness that he felt in the face of Betsy's condition.

In contrast to the darkness in his heart, the trading post glowed warmly with candlelight and a crackling hearth. Slowly, Jake became aware of the smell of venison stew. He hadn't felt hungry until that moment, although it'd been a full day since he'd eaten.

"I'll go wash up and check on the horse," he said quietly.

"I fed and watered him already, Jake. You can give him more, though. He's still acting hungry," McGraw's tone suggested a nonchalance and assurance he clearly didn't feel.

Once outside, Jake revived in the cool night air. Apache, the Arab-quarter horse cross, whinnied demandingly and trotted to the fence in greeting. When Jake'd left Prescott in pursuit of Betsy and her abductor, the horse had still been half wild. In its vigor and drive, the feral mount easily managed seventy miles a day without breaking a sweat, demanding an experienced, strong rider to maintain control. Betsy'd bought this fine stud at auction a few months before. The girl had a natural eye for good livestock, that was certain. Perhaps her idea of raising breeding stock wasn't as silly as he'd then insinuated.

He gently stroked the horse's muzzle as he recalled back to well over a year ago when he'd first stopped at this trading post. Strange, he thought. He'd been hunting Geiger then but hadn't known it at the time, and he'd been trying to forget Betsy, to erase her from his head – and heart. He'd failed at both.

"Well, we found her, Apache," Jake spoke quietly to the horse as he forked an extra ration of hay over the fence. "Not like I hoped, or expected, but we found her." Washing up in tepid water sitting in a basin on the back porch, a sense of starvation and exhaustion nearly swamped him. He realized he'd been tracking either his sister or Betsy for nigh onto almost what, three or four months, living out of the saddle and on what he could shoot or scavenge. He'd stay here for a few days and rest up before this journey's deadly finale. He wanted to be present when the doctor examined Betsy, and he desperately wanted to see an improvement in her before he left on his hunt for the foul perpetrator of this heinous crime, Johnny Geiger. Realizing what he intended, he removed his badge, pocketing it in his vest for the second time since serving as U.S. Deputy Marshal.

Both McGraw and his wife cast baleful glances at Jake throughout the mostly silent meal. Tilly kept forcing food on him until he grew embarrassed. "Jake Silver, I want you to eat every morsel. You look positively haggard, young man."

"Now, Tilly. The man knows when he's had enough," McGraw said, coming to Jake's rescue.

Turning upon her husband, the tiny woman shook her serving spoon at him. "Ben McGraw, you just let me take care of this man. He's going to need every bit of strength he can muster."

Silence fell as each person pondered the meaning of her statement. Finally, McGraw spoke. "Jake, for right now, you need to forget about whoever it is you're after. This isn't the time."

Pushing himself from the table, Jake looked long and hard into McGraw's eyes. The meal had given him a renewed vigor. Power and anger spurred him now, replacing his earlier feelings of sorrow and defeat. "You're wrong, Ben. Now is the time. You don't know this jackal. He's evil. Pure and simple. Rotten through and through. He's known for beating up and abusing women, children, crippled folk. He uses black folk as target practice. His time's up, and I'm the man who's going to end it for him."

"Jake, you're upset. Betsy needs you right now. This isn't the time to take off," McGraw repeated, more forcefully.

"I'll stick around for a few days, but I'm going to end this sooner than later. She'll never be safe…." Jake started to say that their child would never be safe either, but suddenly he stopped, wondering if a baby could withstand what'd just happened to the mother. In the shock of seeing Betsy so battered, he'd forgotten about her pregnancy.

"Is she…is she still…." He paused, uncertain how to ask, his voice breaking.

"What is it?" McGraw asked solicitously.

"Is she still…with child?" Jake asked, fearing the answer he might hear.

"It seems she is," Tilly spoke up. "I didn't know if you knew. The doctor can confirm this, but Shimasani's chants are for the delivery of a healthy boy. The old grandmother refers to him with the Hopi name, Tiponi, Child of Importance."

"My god!" A flood of warmth raced to Jake's face. Would the baby be okay? If Betsy were half dead, how could the baby possibly live? Questions rushed through his mind, but he kept them to himself.

"We'll know when the doctor arrives," Tilly said, reading Jake's face. "My concern at this point, though, is Betsy, not the baby."

Jake nodded in understanding. "I should never have left her." Yet, as he spoke he knew that there'd have been trouble even if he'd been in Prescott simply doing his job. Johnny Geiger brought trouble, pain, and death with him wherever he rode.

"Who is this guy? What happened?" McGraw asked.

"I've been gone a long time," Jake began wearily. "I went to Tombstone to find my sister who's had her own problems. It took me longer than I'd planned to find her and then get her to safety. That's a story for another day, but when I got back to Prescott I found Betsy gone and her ranch hand shot. He may even be dead by now. Geiger left his name and location – taunting me, daring me. He's expecting a final showdown, and he's going to get one that he never imagined."

"So, who's Betsy to you? If'n you don't mind my askin'?" McGraw asked gently.

"I planned on marrying her when I got back to Prescott – if she'd have me. I didn't know she was carrying my child," Jake fumbled for words, bothered that he'd caused Betsy the embarrassment of carrying a child without being rightly married. "Just found out when I got back. Virginia Hall told me. She's taking care of Betsy's ranch hand right now. She's been a good friend, kind of a mother, really, to Betsy since I took Betsy to Prescott after she ran away from the orphan train." Jake paused, then smiled. "That's another long story."

"My my. You do lead an interesting life, Marshal, and have interesting acquaintances! But you're right," Tilly said with matronly concern. "You need to do right by this girl and marry her just as soon's you can. Who do we know can perform this ceremony, Ben?"

"Well, that jackass minister in Freeman could, but he'll never get on out here."

"What about Koteche, Shimasani's husband?"

"Now, Tilly, they don't want to be married by no Indian medicine man. Besides, who'd recognize that as a real marriage?"

"Well, Jake and Betsy would until they could get a preacher in Prescott," the small, feisty woman retorted.

McGraw waved his hand in consternation.

"Well, it's mighty nice that you're both wanting the best for Betsy," Jake said, "but she may not have me after this. She's a pretty independent young woman, and I've come to realize I'm not the best catch. I don't deserve someone as good as her," Jake said, sadness evident in his voice. "My sister recently put me in my place. So did an Apache. I'm not nearly good enough for that girl in there, no matter how much I've come to know that I love her." Jake stopped, his face flushing. He'd never spoken so openly about his feelings. Now he bristled slightly. "Guess we'll see. I'm not putting my hopes on it, but whether she marries me or not, I'll spend the rest of my life making this up to her, that much I swear."

"You're a good man, Jake, but like most men foolish at times. Don't be too hard on yourself. There's hope for you." Tilly smiled kindly, laying her hand on his arm. "Why don't you go on in and stay with her tonight? You've got to be dead tired. I laid some blankets out for you on the floor by the bed. It'll do both of you a world of good to be together."

"Thank you, Miz McGraw. Think I'll do that. You're right. I'm plumb exhausted." Jake stood. "I'm curious how you knew I came here looking for her, though."

"It was writ on your face when you rode up, Jake. Could'a read it a mile away," McGraw said.

Tilly smiled. "What Ben says is true, but she's talked a few times, especially the first night here. That's how we come to know her name, and when she mentioned yours, we knew you'd be coming along."

Jake nodded, hope welling. "Mighty fine dinner. The best I've had since I can't remember when. Thank you both." He paused a moment longer. "I'll never forget that I'm deeply indebted to you. Not sure how I can ever repay you, but know I'll be there if you're ever in need. Ever."

A MAN'S GOTTA DO...

Even before she heard his voice, the familiar footfall announced his arrival. Betsy floated in and out of consciousness and heard only the occasional sound of people's voices, not their words, but when he touched her, the hand felt familiar. She fought to open her eyes, but only one obeyed. Yes, Jake sat by her side, so serious, sadness written on his face and in his posture. *Don't be sad*, she wanted to tell him. *You found me*. She needed him desperately, and he'd come, just like she knew he would. He'd found her, at last, and now she could sleep without seeing the fist streaking toward her. Jake would stop the fist. She wanted only to curl up in his arms and sleep with the beat of his heart in her ears, and the slow, steady warmth of his breath caressing her.

She drifted to sleep yet again, finally relaxing as a sense of peace settled over her. The singing of the old grandmother soothed her, and she sensed a cocoon of safety form. Jake had found her, just like she'd told the nasty, brutal Johnny man that he would. But Johnny, impatient, had hurt her, then dumped her in the desert to die, baking by day, shivering at night. Until the strange men came and took her away – somewhere.

She remembered Indians carrying her to the house of two white people. For awhile she awoke and talked. Something the Indians gave her had revived her, but then she fell asleep, the sleep of death it seemed, and she couldn't awaken. She could smell him now, though, and it was the smell of horse, leather, desert air, and a Jake aroma that made her drunk with happiness.

Unaware of time, Betsy opened her one good eye the next morning to see him on the floor beside her, his face thinner than when she'd said goodbye to him. His whiskered, handsome face and his deep, gentle breathing brought a surge of happiness and strength to her. Even in sleep his strength invigorated her. Involuntarily, her hand went to her swelling tummy. Yes, Jake's baby still lived. She'd protected him from the bad man's blows. She must eat, she realized. The baby needed food. She must get well quickly and regain her strength. She had to go home. Thomas Jefferson, her friend and ranch manager, would need her. That Johnny man had shot Thomas. Betsy needed to help him. The baby had to be born at home. Jake had to take her home. Her mind fluttered with thoughts, worries, dreams.

Suddenly she saw him looking at her, and her small smile in greeting caused her to wince. Her jaw ached. She reached out, and he quickly knelt by her side, pressing her hand to his lips. Neither spoke, each searching for signs of love in the other's eyes.

"Betsy, I love you. I'm here. I'll never leave you again," Jake whispered.

But even as he spoke, a dark realization descended on her, smothering her momentary happiness. No, he would leave, even though he meant what he now said. He would never fully be there with her, and that thought brought tears. She tried to speak but winced in pain when she moved her mouth.

"Don't talk. Your jaw's bruised." He gently raised her to a sitting position, holding her tenderly, but tears of sorrow and fear flowed down her cheeks. Yes, he would leave again…and again.

"He said he'd get you, Jake," she finally managed to mutter. "I'm afraid."

"Shh. Don't you worry none, missy. No one's going to get me. No one's going to hurt you again, you hear me? No one, Betsy." He paused. "I just don't know the words to tell you."

She closed her eye and clung to the thread of happiness he'd offered. She would love him to her dying day, and she understood that he'd love her as best he could. She couldn't ask for more. But all of a sudden a tiny, almost inaudible voice whispered to her that she hated him, and that realization shocked her. She must shut that voice up.

"Take me home, Jake. I want to go home."

"Soon. You need to rest up first. Get better. I'll take you home then. I got a little business to attend to, then we'll leave."

"No, Jake. Take me home now, please." She weakly wrapped her arms about him and buried her face in his neck. "I don't want you going after that man. I need you now! Jake, I'm having a baby. Your baby," she blurted, her jaw aching fiercely. "This isn't how I wanted to tell you."

He smiled at her. "I know. Virginia told me."

"Are you mad?"

"Don't be foolish. 'course I'm not mad! If you'll have me, I want to marry you."

"You're not saying that just because of the baby, are you?" she asked as she laid back on the pillow, another tear trickling down her cheek.

"No. I was gonna ask you the day I got home. I did nothing but think about it the whole time on my way back. It was *all* I could think of," he murmured.

Betsy nodded solemnly. "Of course I'll marry you!" Even as he bent to kiss her gently on the forehead, Betsy felt a fleeting sorrow. Life with Jake would have its challenges and disappointments, most notably his determination to remain a lawman. That's when she saw the vacant spot on his shirt where his badge usually sat.

As though reading her mind, he said, "I took the badge off for now. We'll talk about all that later."

"You took it off because you're going after that man, no matter what I say, aren't you?"

He nodded in response. "A man's gotta do what a man's gotta do, Betsy."

Too weak to argue, she felt herself sinking into slumber. Already he planned to leave her again. He'd just sworn he'd never do so. Another tear slid down her cheek.

***

Dr. Helman arrived that afternoon from Freeman, escorted by two Navajos and McGraw's son, Gunner.

"Marshal Silver. We meet again. You bring me business every time I see you." Doc Helman extended his hand and Jake shook it.

"This here is real serious business, Doc."

"So I gathered from my escorts." Turning to the McGraws, he nodded. "Good day, Ben, Tilly. Good to see you both. So, where's my patient?"

"Right this way. Jake, you just wait right here," Tilly directed. "We don't need men folk in the way right now. In fact, you men skedaddle for a bit."

CANYON OF DEATH

The three men moved to leave, not willing to defy the authoritative Mrs. McGraw. "Let's go on out for a bit, boys," Ben said to Jake and Gunner. Jake suspected that McGraw probably thought it best they not hear any cries of pain. Either that, or he didn't want to defy his tiny wife.

"What kinda horse you got out here, anyway?" Gunner asked, and the men's voices faded as Tilly and Doc Helman entered Betsy's room.

***

"So, what's happened here?" Doctor Helman asked, his eyes widening in surprise as he saw the battered girl before him.

"Well, best we can figure out, she got abducted by some outlaw vermin, beat up, left for dead in the desert, found by the Navajos and treated some by them, then brought here. Jake showed up yesterday searching for her. She's with child, Merton," Tilly said, reverting to her former beau's first name.

"And her?" Merton asked, nodding toward the old Indian woman sleeping on a mat in the corner.

"Well, she's been attending to Betsy – in her way."

"Hmm. Interesting. The Indians give her anything?"

"I'm not sure, but they said they took her to someone's hogan because they didn't think she'd make the trip here without their medicine. She was more communicative and alert when they brought her in. She's been almost comatose since then."

"They probably gave her a stimulant. Maybe some chaparral. Maybe ocotillo wraps. Who knows? Well, let's take a look, shall we?"

Minutes later Merton nodded in approval. "She's got a good strong heartbeat. So does the child. I don't see any broken bones, although she could have a fractured jaw."

"She going to be okay?"

"She's young. She'll heal. It'll take time, but six months from now she should be okay, physically anyway. Not sure how she'll handle this emotionally. Lot of people don't recover from beatings like this."

"How about the baby?"

"Baby seems okay now. We won't know for sure, however, until it's born."

From the corner, the old Indian woman spoke haltingly, "Otekah live. Tiponi live."

"She's saying that Otekah, apparently what she calls Betsy – it means Sun Maiden – will live. Tiponi, Child of Importance, will also live," Tilly explained.

"She some kind of witch?" Merton asked, glancing warily at the old woman.

"A powaga? No. I think she feels that Betsy is her sitsi, her daughter."

Merton turned toward Tilly. "Our patient needs clean water. Food. Broth for a day or two, then you can try something with a bit of meat. Get as much down her as you can. Eggs, if you can muster up any. She needs nourishment, most certainly. I think she should be transported to Freeman as soon as possible. She can stay under my care until she delivers the baby."

"That's a good idea."

"Let's give her another two, three days of rest here. As soon as she's eating and a bit stronger, get her to Freeman. I'll keep a close eye on her, and she can get a more varied diet than what you folks got out here. Not that you're not about the damnedest best cook I ever sampled, Tilly."

Tilly smiled. "I know what you're meanin', Merton. I don't take no offense. I'll have Ben or Gunner transport her as soon as possible."

The two talked quietly in the adjoining room. "I suppose the marshal's going after this Johnny Geiger?" Doc asked.

Tilly nodded. "Naturally. What man wouldn't?" she asked ruefully.

"Bad business, this Geiger. He let everyone in Freeman know he's top dog in this little battle. Jake needs to be careful. Geiger's slick and dangerous. He was in on those girls getting abused a year or so back, you know. Still, if a man's going to ride for revenge, he'd best be sure to dig two graves. Heard that from someone. In my line of work, I see all the time that the saying makes perfect sense."

Tilly nodded. "I well remember. That's the first time we met Jake. He was riding to the rescue then, too." She paused, her brow knitted with worry. "We'll try to keep him here as long as possible. The moment we transport Betsy, though, he might choose to take off then."

"Got any of that good venison stew, Tilly?" Merton asked, abruptly changing the subject. "Traveling makes a man mighty hungry."

CANYON OF DEATH

"Come on and sit right down, Merton. Let me get you some vittles. When are you planning on heading back?"

"I'll stay here today to keep an eye on our little gal, even though I can hardly stand to be around the man who stole my sweetheart," he said, only half-joking.

***

Jake spent the afternoon as he had the day before, holding Betsy's hand, watching her every breath, feeling relief sweep through him each time she opened her eye. Was it his imagination, or did the puffy eye begin to open a tad now also? He noticed that she awoke more frequently and stayed awake a bit longer each time. His confidence in her recovery grew as the day progressed. Greatly relieved by nightfall, he ate heartily, even smiling on occasion at Merton's poorly disguised attempt at flirtation with Tilly.

Talk of transporting Betsy to Freeman finally arose, and while McGraw and his son discussed who'd transport the young woman, Jake remained stonily silent, not offering to accompany them. This would be a good time to go hunting Johnny Geiger, he reasoned, and he wouldn't return empty handed. Jake's silence spoke volumes.

The following day Betsy took her first small meal, and the group sighed with relief when she sat at the table that evening. Although Jake carried her there, she managed to walk back to bed with assistance.

Two days later, Jake laid Betsy carefully on the corn silk filled mattress placed in the wagon for her transport. He sat in the wagon by her side momentarily, but neither spoke of the fact that he would not accompany her, nor of the manhunt which he would immediately begin. Instead, he reassured her of Thomas Jefferson's recovery and about Virginia taking care of things on the ranch. Virginia Hall, a Prescott business woman who ran a top-rated boarding house had been a mother figure to Betsy since Jake had delivered the girl safely to Prescott over a year ago.[1] The tale of the Apache and his sister could wait, Jake reasoned. The Indian was probably in Prescott now, anyway, awaiting his return. Hell, he might even be in Freeman. Jake

---

[1] *Saving Tom Black, Book I of the Jake Silver Adventure Series*

found himself hoping that the Apache would, in fact, show up somewhere along the way.

Jake looked at Betsy and briefly wondered if it was his love for her or his rage at Geiger that drove him. Her disappointment that he would not accompany her showed plainly in her monosyllabic answers and downcast visage. He'd promised he'd never leave her again, but this one time had to be an exception. He couldn't fathom why she failed to understand that. Once he'd wreaked retribution on Geiger, he'd never leave her again. It seemed pointless, however, to repeat what he'd already told her, so he stubbornly refused to say more on the subject.

Finally, Gunner climbed onto the buckboard and gathered the reins. "Okay, Gunner, you take good care of my girl. Betsy," Jake said, leaning over and kissing her on the forehead, "I'll see you in Freeman soon. This won't take long. I promise I'll be there when the baby's born." He spoke confidently, a last-ditch effort to assure her.

She smiled weakly, but doubt clouded her eyes. He inadvertently looked away, momentarily wondering if he ought not accompany her to Freeman, or even take her home where she longed to go. Quickly stepping back, he stood by McGraw as the wagon pulled out. He nodded slightly, his eyes drawn to Betsy, trying to ignore the doubt and turmoil that rumbled in his gut.

"Jake," McGraw began as the wagon pulled away. "Don't mind me sayin', but you're makin' the biggest mistake of your life not goin' with them right now. Trust me. Women don't forget things like this. It's not too late to saddle up and take off after 'em."

"Can't do that. You know that. And believe me, I doubt this is the biggest mistake I've made," he said bitterly.

"Well, come on in then and let's get you some provisions for the trip. You can't live off the land and hunt Geiger, too."

"Thanks. I'll pay you back."

"You keep yourself alive; that's all the payment I'm wantin'."

The two men entered the squat, stone building whose interior seemed cool and dark in comparison to the glaring sun. "You know, don't you, that he ain't up in the big canyon. Gunner said the Indians talked about him bein' run out of there. They said he's headin' down Chiricahua way with some renegades."

Jake halted, surprised. "You sure?"

"Darn sure. Indians wouldn't lie about it. Gotta admit, that's worrisome."

"How would they know?"

"They got ways of knowin' things. You know that by now. They got their ways."

Remembering his encounters with Nantan Lupan, the mysterious Apache that Jake had tracked down to rescue his sister, he nodded. Somehow the people whites considered to be so primitive, had knowledge and ways far more advanced than they were given credit for.

Having heard that Geiger now traveled with a small band of renegades, Jake wished more than ever that Nantan Lupan would appear. He could well use the wily Indian. Probably long since disappeared into Mexico, he mused. The fact that Geiger and his cohorts were in the Chiricahuas, a mountainous, savage region with a bloody history, also concerned him. He didn't know the area at all.

"Stick around tonight, why don't'cha? You can leave at first light. I could use the company. That Shimasani woman makes me right nervous, I gotta say. She's around here someplace with that damn hummin' and chantin'. Spooky, if you ask me. Tilly won't be back til mornin'. She got a yen to visit up Targon way. The Navajos took her. 'Spect she was upset about Betsy and all and you not goin' with her."

Jake nodded, realizing that Ben's request made sense all the way around. He had a lot to do to prepare for the hunt.

The two men spent the afternoon gathering stores and arguing about the various odds and ends Ben insisted were important for the trip, but that Jake argued were an impediment to travel. After much discussion, McGraw persuaded him to take a pack animal. "Jake, you gotta have more provisions than a few tins of beans and some jerky. You're gonna need a lot more water, extra bedding for the Chiricahua area this time of year, extra ammunition, and other stuff."

Reluctantly, Jake agreed, but he worried lest Ben's pack mule get injured or, worse yet, killed. "Cross that bridge when you get to it," Ben replied when Jake voiced his concerns. "Besides, he ain't much for packin'. Hell of a ridin' mule, though."

"It'll be a cold day in hell before I ride a mule," Jake responded.

Good-natured banter flowed between the two men about which was superior, mules or horses.

They talked until late, and Jake filled McGraw in on the recent rescue of his older sister, Sophy. He hesitated to tell of her infatuation with the Apache, but found himself spilling it all. McGraw nodded understandingly as Jake told the tale. "She was out there alone, for months, in this godforsaken hellhole. The only one who came along who was worth a damn was the Indian. I guess they got attracted to each other…somehow.[2] Loneliness, I suppose. He helped her out a lot. Saved her life once. But then he tried to take her with him. That happened after I showed up, during the time all those Apaches escaped from San Carlos."

"Dirty shame things are the way they are," McGraw commented. "Not fair to the Indian, nor anyone else, for that matter. Him getting' shot is a mighty big surprise, though."

"Surprised the hell out of me, too," Jake said.

Finally the story wound down as Jake talked about Peter Burt, the captain who'd ridden out to help rescue Sophy and then become smitten with her, and the return trip to Prescott to find Betsy missing and the ranch manager, Thomas Jefferson, shot. "Jefferson befriended Betsy after she ran away from the orphan train. Helped her disguise herself as a boy so she could travel more safely. That's when I first met her."

McGraw laughed heartily. "I can't imagine her looking anything like a boy."

"She didn't. Piss-poor disguise," Jake said, chuckling at the memory. "Then she inherited a pile of money and a batch of goldmines from her mother's boyfriend. She hired Jefferson to run the ranch when he came looking for her to make sure she was okay." Jake paused. "It's been quite a ride knowing that gal."

---

[2] *Apache, Book II of the Jake Silver Adventure Series*

CANYON OF DEATH

The men turned in long after the mantel clock struck midnight. Both lie awake, troubled and restless. Jake had only a few years on McGraw's own son, Gunner. Jake knew Tilly and Ben had a parental concern and affection for him, almost as much as they did for Gunner. He appreciated their care, yet it annoyed him also. No one seemed to understand that he simply had to do this. For him, no alternative existed, and no one would ever convince him otherwise.

No matter what anyone said, he could not do other than go after Johnny Geiger. Certainly, he would never outdraw Johnny, for the man cleared leather far faster than anyone Jake had ever encountered. If it came to rifles, Jake would win. And if it came to fisticuffs, he would pound Geiger to a pulp, it being only fair after what the cowardly bully had done to Betsy. But in a gunfight, Johnny held the upper hand over most all men – unfortunately.

The two had known each other since childhood days in Fort Worth. It had not been a good time.

GUNNER

Gunner McGraw kept his eyes averted from Betsy the entire first half of the trip from Kaibito, only surreptitiously checking on his passenger as infrequently as he could stand it. He didn't mind escorting the girl to Freeman. Under anything resembling normal circumstances, he wouldn't have minded in the least bit, but these were not ordinary circumstances. The young McGraw vacillated between annoyance, irritation, and worry as the wagon wended along the rutted road.

He'd been at the trading post when the Indians had brought the beaten girl in. It'd physically sickened him to look upon her grotesquely swollen, bruised face. Hunks of hair had been jerked from the girl's head, leaving raw, seeping spots, and her bloody clothing had added to the deeply disturbing sight. Even his parents, frontier people who'd witnessed a lot of man's inhumanity, had expressed shock at the young woman's brutalized appearance.

Riding at breakneck speed to fetch Doc Hellman, the memory of the girl's face made him push his horse to the point of exhaustion. Escorting the doctor back in that slow buggy had nearly driven him to distraction, wondering if the girl yet lived. In his brief absence, the U.S. Deputy Marshal had come. Gunner resented the man. Resented everything about him, though he wasn't exactly sure why. Or maybe he was sure, but didn't want to admit the reason, even to himself.

At twenty-three, Gunner could hold his own with just about any man, or at least he thought he could, and he'd done so on occasion. Smaller than Jake Silver, Gunner had no doubt the marshal could best him in physical combat, but like the marshal, Gunner was long on bravado and short on fear and good sense.

CANYON OF DEATH

Despite the small scar that cut across his right cheekbone, women saw only his dark hair and long-lashed brown eyes. The scar easily served as a conversation starter. After that, Gunner quickly learned to enjoy the ladies.

"Could we stop for just a bit?" the girl lying on the floor of the wagon asked.

"We can stop up yonder by that ridge. There'll be shade," he said, glancing back at her, then quickly looking ahead. After a moment he asked, "Can you make it that far?"

From the corner of his eye, he saw her nod in response. Troubled by the indefinite answer, Gunner turned and fully studied his passenger, questioning if he should stop immediately or continue on.

Two blue eyes, still slightly swollen and blackened, peered at him as she smiled weakly. "Really, I can make it."

He nodded and urged the horses to move a tad faster. "Won't take long," he said.

Thirty minutes later he helped the slight girl from the wagon despite her protestations. "No, ma'am. I got strict instructions from my ma on this matter. I'd sooner take on a passel of Apaches than get her stirred up. She'd scalp me if she found out I didn't help you in every way possible."

Gunner could clearly see the girl's fatigue, yet they still had miles to go before reaching Freeman. He briefly wondered if they should return to the trading post and attempt the journey again in a week or so.

"I'd like you to take me to Prescott," the young woman announced suddenly. "I don't want to go to Freeman. I want to go home. I want my baby born at home. I can make the trip," she added quickly. "I'm not as weak as you think."

Gunner didn't need a doctor to tell him that further travel was out of the question. The girl would never make the trip. "Ma'am, that's about the worst idea I've yet heard in this whole day of bad ideas. I think I best take you back to the trading post for a few more days. Then you can decide where you want to go. You don't look none too well, if you don't mind me sayin'."

He watched as she vainly attempted to stand to her full height, which wasn't all that tall, he decided. Still, he recognized that her attempt showed spirit and determination.

"I'm not going back to the trading post. I'm not going to Freeman. I'm going home. Now. And if you won't take me, I'll walk if need be," she said with more resolve than he thought her capable of mustering in her present condition.

"Where's the next habitation?" she asked, gathering her shawl.

"Just hold on a minute, ma'am," Gunner said, suddenly feeling ill at ease and uncertain how to handle this headstrong lass. He stood a moment, rubbing his chin, studying the small, visibly pregnant girl, wondering what in tarnation to do. He held by his first two choices: return to the trading post or forge on to Freeman where he could turn the little spitfire over to Doc Helman.

"I'm quite well," the girl said in an obvious attempt to speak authoritatively. "I can stand the trip to Prescott, I assure you."

"Ma'am, my instructions are to take you to Freeman. If you decide to go on to Prescott after that, then that's your business. But my business is to take you...."

"You've said that three times now," she interrupted. "And quit calling me ma'am. My name is Elizabeth." She hesitated, then said, "Well, Betsy is what I go by."

Both stood their ground. Finally, Gunner spoke. "Betsy, I'm afraid the trip will be too much for you in your present condition."

"Is that your answer?" Betsy asked disdainfully.

"I'm thinking it is."

"Fine. I'll walk. And don't you dare touch me or try to stop me."

Gunner watched her proceed to walk away and was about to call out when she stopped. "Which way is Prescott, if I may ask?" She turned toward him.

"Never mind. I'll take you if you're that determined." He shook his head in consternation, wishing now he'd insisted that his mother accompany them. She'd know how to handle the situation far better than he. "I suppose we could set up camp here if you don't feel up to travelin' further today," he commented offhandedly. "Let's just camp here for the night and let you rest and think about things. We'll start off tomorrow morning early while it's cool. It could get right chilly here tonight. It's gettin' on towards fall." He hoped that by morning she would come to her senses.

CANYON OF DEATH

"That's a good idea," Betsy responded. "I could use a bit of a rest. I'll be better tomorrow, I assure you."

She perched awkwardly on a large, flat rock, and watched as Gunner unhitched the horses and made camp. Fortunately, they had plenty of water and food. Years of living in the desert had taught the McGraws not to venture out without at least two days' worth of provisions at a minimum. Horses could go lame. Wagon wheels and axles broke. Any number of hazards could come up on a trip, even one of short duration.

"We should probably use the water sparingly. The horses can do without if need be for a day or two," Gunner said.

"You can give them my water," the girl offered.

"No, ma'am. I think you'd best drink all you can. Just don't get to doin' too much other stuff with it."

"Is it safe here?"

"Yes, ma'am. Safe enough, I 'spect."

"Could you please call me Betsy? Ma'am just…just doesn't set well with me."

"Sure. I reckon." Gunner briefly glanced her way as he hobbled the horses, but said nothing for a moment. He found it painful to look at such a young girl so abused…and abandoned…and beautiful. He had to admit that was part of it. Finally, he spoke. "I'm Gunner."

"I know. I heard your mother and father call you so. That's an unusual name, isn't it?"

"Well, it tells a lot about my father, I suppose." Gunner smiled, but quickly corrected himself.

"I'm sorry you're having to take me home, Gunner. It shouldn't be your responsibility to have to do so," Betsy said in a disheartened tone.

"Always wanted to see Prescott," Gunner mumbled after a few moments. "It's my pleasure," he added without much conviction.

He kept the fire low. They had wood in the wagon, but he worried lest they have to make too many stops en route because of her condition, although he expected wood to be plentiful in the Prescott area.

Watching Betsy pick through her food, he could tell she didn't feel well. A Mormon settlement was a good day or two away. He'd stop there and have someone check her to make sure she could continue to travel. He'd have a lot of explaining to do when he got back to the trading post, he suddenly realized. People would panic when it was discovered they'd never arrived in Freeman. How long would it take for them not to show up and the news to get back to Kaibito? he wondered. It was a good 200 miles from the post to Prescott. The more he pondered the distance and Betsy's condition, the more determined he became to hogtie her if necessary and take her directly to Freeman. He'd load her in the wagon in the morning and continue on to Freeman. She'd never know the difference, he reasoned, since she didn't seem to know one direction from the other.

The temperature plummeted as the sun set. Gunner gave Betsy his blanket, now regretting even more the turn of events.

Before dawn, he hitched the horses and began breaking camp while Betsy slept. He didn't see any point in rousing her, but he stowed the coffee pot so she could enjoy a cup of warm coffee upon awakening. Although, if he had to stop as many times again as he'd stopped yesterday for her to relieve herself, maybe the coffee wasn't such a good idea.

Before they'd left, his mother had endeavored to give him a primer on expectant women, and most of it had alarmed him. Having been raised an only child on the frontier, Gunner had seen his share of expectant Indian women, cattle, and horses, but he'd never been privy to the human details.

Despite his plan the evening before to head on to Freeman, Gunner found himself turning the horse and wagon toward Prescott. Damned if he could explain why.

The two traveled in silence a good part of the morning, but finally Gunner said, "So, finish your story about coming West."

"Oh, I don't' know that it's so interesting now that it's daylight," Betsy said, almost laughing.

"No. I'd like to hear," Gunner replied, hoping that talking would keep the girl's mind off the pains that had visited her the night before. "You left off where you headed out from Albuquerque after you bought that horse."

After a few moments, Betsy began. "Well, that's where I met Jake Silver, although I'd seen him much earlier in Topeka, Kansas, in a mercantile. He was heading to Prescott to be the new marshal. We traveled together for a long spell. Once we got to Prescott, he got me settled in Miss Hall's boarding house, then he took off." Betsy paused again as a pained look crossed her face. Gunner studied her carefully, worry gnawing at him. Maybe less talk might be better.

Soon she continued, however, recounting her episode of setting out to look for her mother and finding the woman dead up the Hassayampa River. She'd spent weeks nursing the miner, Shaun Agar, back to health after he and her mother'd been shot by two men whom Jake Silver later killed when he came to find her. Surprised at the wildness of the tale, Gunner said nothing, admiring the girl's daring and also feeling relieved that the trip to Prescott, even in her present condition, paled in comparison to her other adventures.

"That's how I inherited all the money," she said after a spell. "Sometimes I wonder whether it was for the best or not, though."

Gunner remained silent, suspecting that the money might well be the cause of the rift between Betsy and the marshal. He gritted his teeth as he saw a tear slide down her delicate, pale face.

Finally, he asked, "So, Betsy, if you don't mind tellin' me, when is this baby due?" It was the first time he'd mentioned her condition, and he tried not to blush.

Betsy slowly shook her head. "I don't know. I'm ashamed to say I didn't even know I was in the family way for quite a spell. I never had anyone tell me about –" she paused, "about these things."

"Thought you told my folks you wasn't due for a spell," he said, suddenly alarmed.

"I said that. Yes."

"You lied?"

"I might have…overestimated. I don't know, really. I just wanted to go home," she said, turning tear-filled eyes upon Gunner. "Virginia can take good care of me. Thomas Jefferson will help out. It'll be so much better than being with strangers in Freeman."

He found it difficult to be angry when she looked at him with her large, blue eyes and delicate, tear-stained face. Damn. What the hell was coming over him? he wondered. He slapped the horses with the reins to speed them up. It was too late now to turn to Freeman. He'd have to continue on to the Mormon settlement. But what if they didn't make it?

ON THE TRAIL

Just the thinnest ribbon of light lit the eastern horizon when Jake headed out to saddle Apache. Unable to sleep and anxious to hit the trail, he'd arisen and fed the animals at 3:00 a.m., McGraw following only minutes behind.

"Jake, can I talk any sense into that thick skull of yours at all?"

Jake smiled in response and shook his head. "Don't think so, Ben. It's too late for that."

"I can't help feelin' your makin' a big mistake takin' off like this. This isn't a good time. Betsy's in a bad way and could use some of your attention."

Jake remained stubbornly silent as he continued saddling the horse. McGraw sighed in defeat and set about haltering the mule and tying him to the rail. "I got a pack you can use. It's old, but serviceable. Don't fret if anything happens to it."

Jake nodded. "Thanks."

"I'll get the stuff I laid out last night."

Jake watched McGraw as he crossed the patch of hard packed dirt to the back of the trading post. He didn't want to think about McGraw being right. Maybe this wasn't a good time to go on a manhunt, but there was never a good time.

A few minutes later McGraw returned, lugging the heavily laden pack. "Stay on the main roads, will ya? There hasn't been much Indian trouble around these parts for quite a spell, but the farther south you go, the more likely you'll run into a few renegades still roaming around."

CANYON OF DEATH

"I thought they got the last of them when Geronimo turned himself in." Even as he spoke, Jake knew from his first-hand encounter with Nantan Lupan, the renegade Apache his sister had become infatuated with, that Indians still lingered in southern Arizona and northern Mexico.

"Don't count on it. Apaches been roamin' the Southwest for decades. I know for a fact there's still a pack of 'em livin' down in Mexico. Chihuahua. Sonora. They still come and go as they please. So stay on the main traveled roads and you'll be a lot safer."

"Pretty good roads and trails all the way down?"

"Off and on. I recommend when you leave here that you skedaddle on over to the Mormon Wagon Road. It's plenty traveled and follows the Little Colorado River. Small settlements along the way. Got a lot of flat land off and on. That'll help." McGraw paused while he tightened the cinch on the pack saddle. "But you got some real rough travelin', too. Lots of mountains and passes. It's gonna be gettin' cold at the higher elevations this time of year. You're lookin' at 400 miles, anyway." McGraw's voice trailed off, his intention to dissuade Jake all too obvious.

"Then I best get started so I can get back before the snow flies," Jake responded, trying to make light of McGraw's comments.

"Coffee's ready," McGraw said, giving in at last. "Take five minutes 'n have some hot coffee. There's a chill for certain this morning. I got some vittles warming up, too. It'll only take you a few minutes, then you can be off. No point in leavin' hungry. You'll be hungry soon enough, I 'spect."

Jake held a smile in check as he followed McGraw inside.

"I'll draw ya a map as best I can," McGraw offered. "Been that way myself twice. Not all the way to the Chiricahuas, but down as far as Snowflake." After McGraw poured the coffee and set out the food, he took a pencil and paper and began to draw a map.

"Tell me about the Chiricahuas," Jake said.

"I hear it's beautiful country, but rugged as hell. Heard tell of a couple of small towns gettin' started when I was last down in Holbrook. Gayleyville was one. Can't remember the other. Mostly miners. You know how minin' towns can be. Here today, gone tomorrow. Some cattlemen movin' in, so they say. Lots of canyons in the Chiricahuas. Good places for ambush, I might add. Heard there's some rocks down there that are right impressive. Indians call them 'standing up rocks.' Don't know much about all that – just hearsay. But the people I talked to said it's a land both terrible and beautiful. Said once you see it, you'll never forget it. Kinda haunts some, I guess. Or maybe it's lookin' over their shoulders all the time for Indians that haunts 'em."

"So, any folks living in the area?" Jake ignored McGraw's mention of renegades.

"There's some isolated ranches. Small gatherings, I'm thinkin'. Even heard that Johnny Ringo got shot in a place called Turkey Creek down there."

"Wish I had a better map," Jake said, eyeing McGraw's scrawls.

"Well, this one'll do for now. Once you get out of the mountainous region, you're gonna run into lots of flat land again, so that'll make travel easier. Still, you best be real careful travelin' the mountains. Snowflake, Holbrook, Woodruff are all good stops. Somebody there's bound to know the territory. You can re-provision in these places, too. Might get some provisions in Maley, if the town's still there. Pro'bly is, what with the railroad and all. Fact is, I think I heard they were gonna change the name after some general. Anyway, you can always swing by Tombstone, too. It's a coupla days out of your way, but it's a sure thing for supplies. Lots of cowboys down that way roamin' around lookin' for trouble, though. Keep an eye out."

Jake nodded and set his empty cup down. "Well, we could stand around and jaw about this all day long, Ben. I best be going if I'm going."

"Well, I'll see ya off," McGraw answered, putting on a coat.

"What's the mule's name?" Jake asked as he mounted Apache.

"I call him Wild Bill. You'll find out why soon enough," McGraw said as he handed the lead line to Jake. "You take care. Make tracks back as soon as your business is done down there. We'll look in on Betsy every time we get to Freeman."

Jake nodded and headed Apache south, Wild Bill braying in protest.

Betsy. Why had he not thought of her even once this morning? His stomach churned, and he pushed worrisome feelings of her away as he looked into the slowly lightening horizon. "Beautiful morning, Apache.

Let's see if we can get Wild Bill to move on out a bit." The horse snorted, the mule brayed, but both picked up their pace.

Travel through the Navajo Reservation was much as McGraw had described. Quiet. Fairly flat. Dry. Only one good rain swept the area, not really a monsoon since it was so late in the season, and both Jake and the animals welcomed the downpour. Water pooled for a brief spell, but lasted long enough for the trio to hit the Little Colorado River.

Despite the sparse population, Jake kept an eye out for likely places of ambush. The few Indians he encountered sullenly glared at the lone traveler. With each encounter, Jake expected trouble, but none occurred. He avoided the Mormon residents as much as possible, and they seemed to avoid him also. He looked serious and deadly. And he was.

He approached the natives at a trading post north of Holbrook, and both they and the trading post owner, John Merriman, recalled seeing a few white men traveling through a while back, accompanied by some renegades. The Indians claimed livestock had been taken by the men, along with a Navajo girl.

"The missing girl, a shideezhi, younger sister to a Navajo leader, has stirred these folks up a bit. Best be careful. We'll spread the word you're lookin' for the girl's captors, but word don't always spread well in these parts," Merriman said. "Why you lookin' for these outlaws, anyway? You ain't one of 'em, are you?"

"Hardly." Jake pulled his badge from his vest pocket and laid it on the counter for the trader to inspect.

"Good idea not to wear this openly," the man commented. "Hard to say how the locals might react, given the situation."

Jake nodded and re-pocketed the badge. "Mind if I sleep out back tonight?"

"I can do you one better. Why don't you join me? Have a bite to eat. Bet ya haven't had a good home-cooked supper in a spell. Rest a day or two before you head on. Your animals look like they could use a day or two off the trail, if you don't mind my sayin'."

Jake mulled the offer over. He wanted to stay, but Merriman had stoked the burning urge to kill Geiger. Still, a day's rest might mean he could make better time later when it might become urgent to pick up the pace. "Thanks," he finally said. "I'd be right glad to accept your invitation."

"I don't get lots of white folks here. It'll be good talkin' with you," the merchant said. "I'm still none too good at this Navajo talk."

For the first night since leaving Kaibito, Jake slept soundly, knowing the animals were well secured in the corral and that the chance of attack was remote.

Even after dozing most of the next day sitting in the sun on the post's front porch, Jake's fatigue only seemed to grow. Maybe another day's layover wasn't such a bad idea. He'd been on the trail for weeks – no, months. He'd left Prescott to look for Sophy in late July, or was it early August? It seemed so long ago. It had to be mid-October now. McGraw was right. October might prove to be awful late to be heading through the mountains. Still, the weather seemed moderate enough. He'd rest one more day and then make up for lost time once he hit the trail again.

He re-shod Apache in the afternoon and checked Wild Bill's hooves. The mule had proved worthwhile. Despite his reluctance to take the animal, Jake recognized the critter's value. Far stronger than a horse and more surefooted, the animal traveled tirelessly, carrying its load effortlessly. So far Wild Bill had been cooperative and agreeable, laying to rest Jake's erroneous belief of mules being stubborn, ornery critters. Merriman, taking quick notice of the animal, offered to buy him.

"Not mine to sell," Jake answered. "Belongs to a friend."

"Must be a good friend," Merriman commented. "That's a fine animal."

That night over a bowl of venison stew, Jake questioned the trader about travel to the Chiricahuas on the offhand chance the man might be familiar with the area. Merriman astounded Jake with his knowledge.

"From here you're gonna keep on the road 'til you hit a new Mormon settlement called Snowflake. It's a good place to stop if you've a mind to. Safe enough. I'm thinkin' you can get a room, maybe so. From Snowflake south, though, the travelin' gets a bit rough for quite a spell." Merriman stopped speaking while he sopped up gravy with a chunk of biscuit.

"What do you mean by rough?" Jake asked.

"From Snowflake there's a road that heads southeast – don't remember what it's called, but it'll get ya on down to Fort Apache. Haven't traveled that route myself, but I've heard it's decent enough. Once you're down in that area a bit, there's usually plenty of water in the rivers and streams."

"Isn't that taking me out of my way?" Jake asked.

"Only a bit. The only other alternative is to strike off over the mountains. Wouldn't recommend that this time of year. Or, you can travel a far piece out of yer way by headin' due West for quite a spell, then cuttin' south. Yer gonna run into some mountain area no matter which way ya go, though," Merriman said.

Jake sighed heavily. A nagging thought that maybe he should return to Freeman began to pester him. He quickly ignored the idea. "Okay. So I get to Fort Apache. Then what?"

"From there on there's trails and wagon roads real regular goin' in all directions. I'll draw ya up a map tonight as best as I can recollect. Once ya get to Fort Apache, though, it's mostly easier travelin'. Ya might even tag along with soldiers headin' yer way. The problem, see, is that while the roads are plentiful, so are the Apaches…still."

"Good advice," Jake said, not at all certain that he wanted to travel with a troop of soldiers. He didn't want to see Indians killed. "I'll sure appreciate any kind of map you can put together."

"It's late for travelin' some of this area, but once yer south of Ft. Apache a way, chances are ya won't see any snow to speak of. It can get cold. You got extra blankets and a heavy coat?"

"I do," Jake said. "I got more stuff on that mule than I'll use in a year, I think."

"Never hurts to have extra. You can always trade with folks, you know."

Jake nodded, suddenly fatigued at the thought of the miles that still lay ahead. Maybe his full stomach made him feel tired.

"You look plenty beat, Jake. Whyn't you get some sleep? I'll get that map drawed and have it for ya in the mornin'. I been south of Ft. Apache a ways. Not as far as Maley, but I remember that area clear enough," Merriman stated confidently.

"Thanks. Think I'll turn in here in a bit after I check on the animals. I got some long days ahead of me," Jake said, rising and putting on his coat, fighting the temptation to curl up by the fireplace.

"Once ya get to Maley, I ain't got any idea how ya get to the Chiricahuas," Merriman continued, clearly enjoying his expertise. "They lie about 40 miles south, is all I know. Not familiar with that area at all. I'm sure you can find someone in Maley who can help you out, though. There's a fort not too far from there. Can't remember the name right off. But that'd be a good place to get reliable information, I'm thinkin'."

The cool air immediately revived Jake, and he decided to remain outside for a bit. Though tired, he didn't want to sleep yet. He fought indecision. If he was going to turn back, this would be the place to do so. Yet, the idea of turning back seemed repugnant, his determination to get Johnny Geiger too strong for him to think objectively. Was McGraw right? Should he be with Betsy and leave this undertaking for another day? He refused to think about the matter further, stubbornly putting it from his mind.

Jake saddled and mounted at daybreak, the chill in the air now undeniable. Ahead, all he could see was the ink-blue outline of jagged, distant mountains. Even more mountains lay beyond, until finally the Chiricahuas rose, beckoning him to his death, or to retribution.

HOMEWARD BOUND

Gunner tried to hide his unease. He could see that Betsy desperately fought to not show the pains she often felt. Though unfamiliar with matters of childbirth, he suspected she had not been in her condition long enough to deliver a healthy baby. Perhaps the pains were due to the jarring of the wagon, he told himself, or perhaps from her unhappiness at the marshal abandoning her. Either way, he didn't care. He shouldn't even be here with her.

The hours traveling seemed endless, although he saw that the two days they'd rested at the Mormon settlement had helped her regain some strength. He'd watched as the Mormon women tirelessly fussed over her, pleading with her not to continue the journey until her time of confinement was over. He'd hoped she'd listen to reason, but knew better than to bet on it. At one point, he'd worried they might even try to keep her against her will, so determined were they that she should not be traveling in her condition. Matters grew only worse when he inadvertently revealed that he was only her escort, not her husband. No further questions were forthcoming about the baby's parentage, and from that moment on he read disapproval in everyone's eyes. He found himself hating Jake Silver for compromising the girl. Her own complicity toward her condition didn't enter his mind.

"Betsy, we have a day to Tuba City," he told her the second afternoon of their stay. "From there it'll be three or four days to Prescott. Can you make it?" Gunner asked. He'd not been allowed to visit her once the fact that they weren't married had been discovered, so they quietly spoke on the porch of the large house.

CANYON OF DEATH

"Yes. I need to get out of here, Gunner. Let's leave tomorrow. Early. We can stay over in Tuba City for a day if needed," Betsy said anxiously.

"You won't want to stay in Tuba City. Trust me. I've been there. It's not a safe place for someone…like yourself," Gunner stammered, hoping she wouldn't notice his cheeks redden. "Besides, I don't have any extra money on me. Wasn't planning on going all the way to Prescott when we left the post."

"I've got lots of money, Gunner. I don't have it on me, but whatever you spend, I can pay you back."

"I'll hitch up the horses early and drive around to the front. You be ready to go, first light," he said, looking away. "Are you sure, Betsy, that you're able to do this?"

"Yes! And thank you, Gunner. I know this hasn't been easy for you. I'll make it up to you somehow. I promise."

After leaving the Mormons as planned, the trip grew interminable. The weather grew colder, and Betsy fainted twice. Gunner cursed under his breath for minutes at a time, frustrated and angry that he'd let himself be persuaded by the girl. Although plenty old enough, he still dreaded hearing his mother deride him for the stupid decision he'd made when he returned home. His father would give him a surreptitious wink. The older McGraw knew Gunner became putty in the hands of a good-looking woman, and that's exactly what had happened to him with Betsy.

The roads being good and a few ranches and way stations available now, at least accommodations for the last portion of the trip were passingly fair. Though the two had no money, no person was hard-hearted enough to turn the expectant girl and young man away. Despite traveling ten or more hours a day, the distance to the mountains adjacent to Prescott never seemed to diminish. Even their approach to the San Francisco peaks, a landmark Gunner had chosen, seemed to tease him by always remaining just beyond reach.

"It's not much farther," Betsy announced one morning. "We're almost to Prescott. We'll be at my house today," she said, smiling for the first time in a week.

Gunner nodded. Relief rushed through him, and he inadvertently smiled back. "Good," he said, almost joyously. "Glad to know that baby is going to be born in a bed and not the back of a wagon,"

For the first time in days the two talked, both thankful and pleased that the trip was almost over. "I can't wait to be home," Betsy said. "You'll never know how much this means to me, Gunner. There's no way I can ever repay you for what you've done for me. Oh! I'll give you some money for your time and expenses. Don't worry about that, but I can never give back what you've given me by bringing me home," she said, smiling happily.

Gunner blushed, his past anger dissolving in the dimples on her cheeks. "My pleasure, Betsy," he said, reddening even more. "I gotta admit I'll be real relieved once you're safe and sound.

"I want you to stay for a few days, if you would," Betsy continued. "I hope you won't mind, will you? Staying for just a bit? Until I get situated and everything's okay?"

Gunner nodded in response. He hadn't given much thought to staying on, but the moment she mentioned it he realized he'd planned on it anyway. He couldn't go off and leave her until he knew she had someone there to look after her and take care of her.

"I'll send a wire to Freeman," Gunner said. "Tell them what's happened. I'm sure they're wondering where in tarnation we are. Probably worried sick about us."

"I don't think so," Betsy answered, looking down guiltily at her hands folded in her lap. "I left a note. I told your folks that I was going home, one way or the other. I'm sure they found it and figured out what happened."

Gunner sighed and shook his head in disbelief. "You should've said something way back on the trail. I been worried about my folks worryin' about us."

"I'm sorry, Gunner."

He could see that the girl had a mind of her own and wanted her own way, at any cost. He should've seen that in the story she told about leaving Prescott and striking out on her own to look for her ma. A foolhardy tale if he'd ever heard of one. He briefly wondered if the marshal had problems with some of the girl's stubborn, head-strong traits.

CANYON OF DEATH

The sun had long since set when the wagon drew up in front of Betsy's log home. Gunner sat, amazed at the ponderous log structure. Although dusk prevented him from seeing the entire property, the sheer size of the home indicated the acreage and accoutrements of the property would be equally as impressive.

Helping her from the wagon, he heard the sound of footsteps on the massive front porch. "Who's there? Jake? Is that you?" a woman's voice called.

"It's me! Betsy!"

"Oh, my Lord! Betsy! Child, is that really you?" the woman said in a breaking voice. "Oh, praise the Lord!" They heard footsteps running across the porch and down the steps.

The next moment, a tall woman threw her arms about the girl, kissing her on the forehead, crying out her name in disbelief. "Betsy! Betsy! Oh my poor girl! Are you okay? Come! We must get you inside quickly. And who's this with you? You, sir, come in also."

Gunner stood awkwardly in the large room as the older woman sobbed and hugged Betsy for what seemed an interminable amount of time, weeping in joy at seeing her and in sorrow because of her ugly mending bruises. The two embraced warmly, oblivious of his presence. He shifted uneasily from foot to foot, wondering how he might best extricate himself from this unexpected, emotional homecoming. He wanted to tend to his team, but hesitated lest his movement stop the celebration.

Finally, the woman released Betsy and looked him over, her eyes still streaming tears. "And who do I have to thank for returning Betsy?" she asked, dabbing at her tears with the corner of her apron.

"This is Gunner McGraw, Virginia. His father owns the trading post where the Indians took me after they found me in the desert. His parents saved my life. Gunner brought me home."

"Oh, my dear! I cannot believe that you made this trip in your condition!" Virginia said, both astonishment and disapproval evident in her manner.

"I insisted. I wanted to come home, Virginia. I just wanted to come home," Betsy said, beginning to sob again. "Gunner, this is Virginia Hall. She's my friend – and my mother."

Gunner wondered how much longer the theatrics in the room could last. "Excuse me, ladies, but I best put my team up. They've had a long trip. If you don't mind, I'll take a lantern down and put them away for the night."

"Of course. I'm sorry to leave you standing there," Virginia said. "Take care of your horses, and by then I'll have some food ready for you. Neither of you look any too well."

Despite her exhaustion, Betsy sat up late talking with Virginia after Gunner excused himself in an attempt to give the ladies a chance to be together. It was plain that Betsy needed Virginia far more than she needed him at this moment. And exhaustion overwhelmed him now that he finally had the girl delivered, safe and sound, against all odds. Never again, he vowed as he lay his head on the soft, feather pillow. Never again. He slept instantly.

Gunner awoke early and lay for a few moments in the feather bed, taking in what seemed to him sumptuous furnishings and decor. Having been raised in a trading post and the back of a wagon, it didn't take much to impress him, and Betsy's home definitely impressed him. He could almost understand why she'd been so insistent about returning. He heard the clang of kitchen pans and finally arose, reluctant to wear his trail-dusty clothing for yet another day.

Following a succulent breakfast, at Virginia's insistence hot water was drawn, and after a long bath and shave, Gunner emerged to find a pile of men's clothing neatly stacked in his room. Probably Jake Silver's, he mused. The clothes were a bit large, but certainly serviceable. He'd get his own clothing back as soon as possible. He didn't like the idea of wearing Silver's clothing, particularly since it emphasized his smaller size.

He didn't see Betsy that day, or the next. Or the next. Finally, not wanting to appear interested or nosy, he mentioned her absence to Virginia Hall. "She took a bad spell when I told her that Thomas Jefferson died," Virginia said, her eyes welling. "Happened a week or so ago. I had him buried out in the orchard like Marshal Silver asked. He was a lovely man. Over a hundred people came to pay their respects. I know he died with Betsy on his mind. He doted on her. We all do. You will, too, if you stick around long enough, although I'm sure you'll want to leave when the marshal returns." She paused, then asked, "Do you have any idea when he might be coming back?"

"I only know the fool man went after an outlaw instead of taking care of…her," Gunner said, trying to mask his disdain.

Virginia said nothing for a bit. Finally, she asked, "Would you mind terribly staying until he returns? The place is in bad need of a hired man. I simply cannot do the work, nor obviously, can Betsy. She could use a good ranch hand right now. Just until the marshal comes, mind you. We wouldn't expect you to stay longer. Betsy will pay you handsomely, I know. And we'll want you to take a room here on the property in case that bad man returns." She paused for a few moments. "Will you consider our proposal?"

"I can stay for a bit, I suppose. Just until she gets on her feet…and the marshal returns," Gunner said, wondering why he was staying when Virginia could easily hire a man from town. "Does Betsy know about this arrangement, or is this your idea?"

Virginia shook her head. "After I told Betsy what all has gone on, she wanted someone immediately. Her thoughts turned to you almost at once. I do hope you'll help her out, Gunner."

Gunner nodded. "Well, in that case I best go and check things out, I suppose. Maybe you can fill me in on what's gone on and, more importantly, what's gone wrong. That would save a passel of time."

"We can talk at lunch," Virginia said, releasing a pent up breath of worry and showing signs of relief. "I'll stay with her here also," she added. "She shouldn't be alone, and I don't want people to talk more than they already do." A look of dismay passed over her visage. "I also want to know what's happened to her. She looks frightful, all bruised and…well, she looks quite dreadful."

"You have no idea what dreadful looks like, ma'am," Gunner replied. "And you don't want to know."

It didn't take Gunner long to recognize that his work was cut out for him. He turned his two horses onto the pasture where several others roamed. The grass looked dry, but he'd have to watch the animals for founder, anyway. Saddling one of the ranch horses, he rode the fence line and learned the acreage was small, at most a hundred acres total. The fence line looked good, although it was down in two areas. He propped the leaning posts up, wondering how many livestock had wandered off. Probably few, if any, he reasoned, since good feed and water had been available. Despite the lateness of the season, a few cows looked ready to drop, and he wondered if he'd have to pull any calves, something he'd had no experience at. She shouldn't have let cows breed off season, he thought. But, what would she know about such things? That was a man's realm, wasn't it?

After lunch he told Virginia he wanted to ride into town to send a wire to Freeman informing his parents of his plan to stay for a bit. "Is it far to town?" he asked.

"Perhaps ten miles at most," she answered. "While you're there, would you mind retrieving Betsy's horse from the stables? She's asked about him three times."

"Her horse? What's it doing there?"

"Jake left it when he returned from his last trip. She'd like to have the horse here. Would you mind doing that?"

"No, ma'am. That's why I'm here. To help however I can."

"Here's money for the horse's board. I'll write out a note in case they question why you're taking him. Everyone knows the horse belongs to Betsy," Virginia said matter of factly. "It's a long story."

"That girl has a lot of mighty long stories, if you ask me."

Virginia smiled, "Yes, I suppose she does. Having a baby will settle her down, though."

I doubt it, Gunner found himself thinking.

The trip to town was pleasant. He enjoyed the turning leaves, something not seen on the high desert, and it felt good to actually ride a horse again, instead of drive one. Wire sent, he found the livery and paid the stablemaster for the animal's keep. "You be careful. That thing done gone plain wild," the owner of the livery commented. "I'm telling you, I think he's reverted back to his wild days. Never seen nothin' like it. Calm one day, crazy the next."

"Could he have gotten into some loco weed?" Gunner asked.

"Don't see how. Just be forewarned. Crazy bastard horse."

"Maybe bein' in a small pen doesn't suit him," Gunner offered, hopefully.

CANYON OF DEATH

"Hmmph. Well, you tell Miss Betsy to be right careful if she's thinkin' of ridin' this devil. She shouldn't ride him at all. I'm tellin' ya, the horse is loco. You be careful leadin' him," the man continued. "Hate to see anyone hurt, especially her. Nice little gal. Say, how's she doin', anyway?"

"She'll live. She's got good care now," Gunner said.

"The marshal come back with her?"

"No. I did," Gunner replied through gritted teeth.

"Well, he sure ain't around much anymore. Always off chasin' one thing or another. Not sure he's meant to be the settlin' down type. But, it ain't any of my business anyway."

"You're right," Gunner said, wanting to change the subject.

"You just be careful. Don't go lettin' her ride this animal till someone who knows horses works him over."

HELL BENT

Apache and Wild Bill alerted Jake to the presence of others long before the intruders notified him of their presence.

"Hello the camp!" a solitary man spoke, almost quietly, but Jake heard the breathing of several mounts. Had it not been for the utter silence of the night, punctuated only by the occasional snap of a sap-covered piece of wood in the fire pit, the voice might have gone undetected, or been misidentified as simply one of those strange night sounds.

"State your business," Jake responded, moving farther from the fire. He knew the night riders had spread out, and by watching Apache's and Wild Bill's ears and their interest in the wooded area, he also suspected he knew where each man hid. By his reckoning three lie hidden, and one approached. Why did outlaws run in packs? he wondered. They rarely traveled alone, and almost always had more than one companion in tow. "Tell your friends to come on around and enter behind you."

A moment of silence ensued, then came the whispering and rustling of pine boughs. "There's three of us. We'll come in slow."

"No, all of you better come in, or I'll be shooting into the brush," Jake answered, gambling the group had more than three riders. He heard more whispering. "Better yet, why don't you boys just ride on by. I'm not feeling too hospitable tonight." Jake slowly cocked the shotgun, and the clicking of the mechanism silenced the group. Nobody ever mistook the metallic click-click of a shotgun. The unpredictable scatter effect of shotgun shells intimidated and often proved deadly. Jake slipped fully into shadows cast by the pine.

CANYON OF DEATH

Now a longer silence reigned. Finally, he heard hooves departing, but he recognized there weren't enough hooves to match up with the four horses he'd been certain were present. Maybe only three men had attempted to ride in, he considered, but he quickly dismissed this notion. He grew irritated knowing it'd be a long, tiresome night. Now that intruders had tried to enter his camp and had been rebuffed, they'd probably try to sneak back if they were of the criminal variety. If just late night travelers, they'd move on begrudgingly. Jake didn't take to the notion of allowing more than two travelers to share his campsite. One against two was manageable; one against four could get dicey. Only trouble stirred about this time of night, anyway.

After waiting five minutes, he moved to extinguish the dying fire. Two shots rang out, one whistling past his ear, the other sinking into the downed tree behind him. "That's it," he mumbled. "Those bastards have ruined my night!"

Rather than retreat, Jake simultaneously scattered the embers and burning sticks and fired in the direction from which the shots had come. Almost immediately he heard someone yell and curse. He knew his attackers would experience a moment of night blindness if they'd been looking at him by the fire. Taking advantage of this, he whirled about, pumped another shell into the shotgun's chamber, and fired in the opposite direction. Although he missed hitting the outlaw behind him, he clearly heard the man's frantic movements through the pine boughs and scanty brush. This time Jake drew his Colt and fired in the vicinity of the shaking brush. A dull thud and groan convinced him the shot had been a lucky one and had hit the target. Quickly but cautiously, Jake headed in the direction of the fallen man. This approach was dangerous because the criminal might still be capable of squeezing off another shot, but darkness and the element of surprise sided with Jake. The man most likely would never expect anyone to approach.

A voice from the other side of the small clearing rang out. "Potter, you hit?"

"He's dead all right," Jake yelled back. "And waiting for you to join him in hell."

A steady drone of cursing and expletives ensued as two gunmen trotted off, leaving their dead and wounded behind.

Jake slowly circled to the area where he'd fired the first shotgun blast. He stopped, listening closely for the sound of labored breathing. Almost immediately he heard the wounded man's whimpering and moans and moved toward him, gun cocked.

"Don't shoot!" the man sniveled. Then, in a surge of bravado he said, "You bastard. I shoulda killed ya when I had you dead to rights."

Jake knelt, trying to peer into the man's face, but shadows and darkness limited his vision. "Who are you?"

"None of your business, that's who I am."

"Just asking, so I know what name to put on your grave marker."

"You can't kill me. You're a law man. You gotta take me in. The law says."

"What makes you think I'm a lawman?" Jake asked, genuinely curious.

"The man at the trading post spilled his guts after we…" the outlaw halted. "You gotta abide by the law, Mr. Big Man Marshal Jake Silver."

"See this badge?" Jake asked, pulling the tin star out of his vest pocket and dropping it into the dirt.

The whites of the outlaw's eyes widened in surprise.

"Guess you won't have a name on that marker. Tell you what. I won't even bury you. I'll let the animals scavenge your corpse. How's that?" Jake stood, pointing the Colt at the man's head.

"Mister. I'm sorry. Real sorry. It wasn't my idea. It…."

The Colt's loud explosion silenced the would-be killer.

"Bad timing on your part, stranger," Jake said to the corpse. "I'm not in the mood to put up with you."

Jake moved back to the campsite. He'd have to let the fire die out completely – no use making himself an easy target if the remaining two outlaws returned. He doubted they would, but still…. A sigh of resignation escaped him. The night would be damn cold. Fortunately, he had plenty of blankets, thanks to Ben McGraw's insistence. Had it not been for the extra blankets, however, Jake would not have taken the route over the mountains instead of the road he'd been advised to take. Had he not taken this route, perhaps two men might still be alive. He fretted about the fate of the trading post owner. Another person dead perhaps, because of him?

The mountainous route was as rugged as any, and certainly no easier. Indian and animal trails made the going a bit faster at times, but the isolation of the area haunted him. He felt watched, yet neither of the animals had given any indication that any living creature was around and, while Jake didn't know about mules, he knew that horses had good senses for detecting people and other animals. Twice, however, Wild Bill inexplicably went into a braying, bawling, bucking fit. The first time he'd jerked so unexpectedly and forcefully on the lead line that Jake's middle finger had been painfully pinched between the line and Apache's saddle horn. Only the snapping of the line spared the finger from being literally pinched in two. Swollen, black, and misshapen, the finger's appearance and continued throbbing let him know it was broken. Of course, Apache had insisted on putting on a show of bad behavior in conjunction with Wild Bill's display.

Wild Bill's second outburst resulted in the mule's escape and Jake having to track the animal down, which had taken the better part of two hours. Perhaps the mountainous, forested area spooked the mule also.

After leaving the trading post, the trip had gone exactly as Merriman had described. He'd easily reached Holbrook, then Snowflake, by keeping to fairly well-traveled roads. It was at the last stop that he met an old timer who insisted the trail over the mountains would save time, and the man had drawn a map of sorts, although the old miner thought he excelled in verbal directions.

"Now, yer gonna head south, so keep that in mind. Get yer bearins' in the mornin' at sunup. That's east, in case ya mighta forgot. Now, yer gonna head south. In a bit, you'll come to a big rock sittin' up on a cliff. Looks like a big rock. Just keep on goin'. Keep that to yer right. A bit later...." And so the narrative had gone. Overall, and despite the long, drawn-out description of the trip, it hadn't sounded all that difficult.

And now this. Two men dead, and maybe Merriman lay dead also back at the post. Jake hadn't counted on anyone else using this route south this late in the year. At least, he thought, brightening for a moment, he'd have good tracks to follow in the morning – assuming the two outlaws headed south and not to some lair.

Despite his intention to stay alert, he slept for a few hours. The rustling of the animals awoke him well before the weak sunlight penetrated the deeply forested pass. A gray cast to the sky told him, however, that dawn would soon break. With no fire over which to cook, he packed Wild Bill, saddled Apache, and was ready to leave in short order. Before mounting, he inspected both men he'd killed the night before. One, grizzled and rough looking – the one apparently called Potter – had seen better days. The other outlaw had died too young, his smooth cheeks attesting to his youth and explaining the smart-aleck attitude. Only a kid or someone with a death wish would be stupid enough to sass a man pointing a gun.

Jake's stomach turned when he saw the boy. Guilt momentarily flooded through him, but quickly bitterness and anger overtook the softening emotions guilt evoked. "You ride with outlaws, you die with outlaws," Jake mumbled as he turned away and mounted Apache. He spun the horse sharply about, untied Wild Bill, and pushed both animals into a jog. He thought briefly of his encounter with the four outlaws he'd killed while traveling in the Mazatzals. "Can't keep doing this," he said aloud. "Johnny'll be the end of the line for me. No more." Even as he spoke, he somehow sensed the end would only come when he himself would be lying in the dirt. What would happen to…he shut the question out before he finished asking.

The route through the mountains, he soon realized, might be shorter than the wagon road, but it wouldn't gain him any time unless he could somehow pick up the pace. One more fit from Wild Bill, though, and he'd be traveling with one animal. That might help. Would the mule find his way back to McGraw's if he cut the animal loose? Someone would claim the surly critter, at least for awhile.

"If you're going with me, no more attitude, Bill. You got that?" As though acquiescing, the animal picked up its pace and trotted along amiably.

The trail left by the outlaws headed south, and it quickly became apparent they'd ridden this direction before. They took little shortcuts Jake would not have discovered, so preoccupied was he with his current mission and just finding his way. Some of the trail looked like it dead ended in a rock wall, but always the path led on. He rode warily, keeping a watch for the miscreants of the night before. He didn't want to unexpectedly ride into their encampment.

The day passed. The next day passed. Finally, the trail began to almost imperceptibly descend. He traveled occasional ascents, but always the uphill sections quickly led to a descent. Even though there'd been no sign of his attackers, Jake remained on guard. He knew attacks inevitably came when one least expected them. It was a rule. A law. A man could count on it, and the West was scored by the graves of men who forgot this rule.

The fourth day he hit the main trail, or at least a well-traveled one. He couldn't keep a smile of relief from crossing his face, but he kept in mind the necessity of keeping an eye out for possible attack.

That night another visitor approached. "Hello to the camp," a cheery voice sang out. The man sounded friendly, trustworthy, and Jake found himself responding accordingly.

"Come on in, mister. Keep your weapon holstered," he added.

"Don't carry no weapon, sir. I trust in the Lord and the inherent goodness of man," the stranger replied.

Jake stood silent, waiting to see what such a wholesome-thinking fellow might look like. In rode a short, stocky character who had the look of a farmer about him. A smile seemed permanently plastered to the man's friendly face. Despite the plainness, even impoverished appearance of his garb, his horse appeared well fed and cared for.

"My name's Silas. Silas Emile Munsey," the man announced. "I come from San Simon down yonder, south of here. Heading that way. Returning just now from Snowflake. Where you from? If I may be so bold to ask." His easy manner was unmistakable, and Jake marveled that such a traveler in these parts remained alive.

Jake studied the curious, pleasant man before him. "You're one lucky son of a gun to be alive if you go around trusting everyone," Jake commented.

Munsey smiled and nodded. "So some say. But the Lord looks after His sheep, of which I'm one."

"My name's Jake Silver. Most recently from Prescott."

"Would that be Marshal Jake Silver?" Munsey asked, dismounting. "I've heard about you. Good things, I assure you."

Jake nodded, surprised that the man knew of him. "What do you have there?"

"I'm bringing a pup home for my son," Munsey answered, taking a small, black dog from his saddlebag. "The boy's been wanting a pup for some time. Can't wait to see his expression when he sees this little guy. My Davey is six years of age this month."

The nondescript puppy yipped and uttered a solitary, tiny bark. Jake could imagine a little boy thinking the dog to be the most wonderful gift in the world. "I'm sure he'll like it," he said. "Well, unsaddle and make yourself comfortable, Mr. Munsey. I'll get you a stick so you can roast your own venison steak over the fire."

"Mighty kind, Marshal Silver. I haven't had fresh meat in quite a spell."

"I shot the buck this afternoon. Just call me Jake, by the way. I'm not here on official business." Despite his curiosity as to how Munsey knew he was a marshal, Jake resisted the temptation to question him, and was quickly rewarded with an unsolicited explanation.

"Yes, indeed. I stopped at Merriman's post a few days back. He told me to keep an eye out for you. Told me you were a marshal. Out here on a manhunt."

"He's quite a talker," Jake responded, disappointed that Merriman'd told Munsey information Jake would rather have kept private.

"Well, I happened on him after some ruffians beat him up quite badly. Pistol whipped the poor man. Left him bleeding from every orifice on his head. Broke some of his bones. He was in a bad way, but the Indians seemed to be taking care of him okay. He told me if I saw you to warn you about the four men. Naturally, I asked who you might be that must be warned. That's when he said you were the territorial marshal. Told me to tell you that the ruffians were riding to join up with…." Munsey suddenly stalled, searching his memory.

"Johnny Geiger?" Jake offered.

"Yes! By golly! That was the name!"

Jake nodded and smiled weakly. "Yep. Got me an appointment with that man."

"Sounds serious, Marshal. I'll pray for your safe deliverance," Munsey said earnestly.

CANYON OF DEATH

The man soon tore into his steak which still remained largely raw despite his having waved it around in the fire for a considerable spell. Silence prevailed as he inhaled the piece of meat. During this time Jake lounged about, relaxing much more than he had in evenings past. Even though Munsey didn't carry a weapon, his company had a soothing effect.

Finally Jake spoke. "So, you know the territory well, Mr. Munsey?"

"Silas, please. No formality with me. As to the country, I'd say I know it fair to middlin'. Been living in the San Simon area quite a spell. Now that the Indian raids have died down we're enjoying it much more. My wife still talks about going back to Arkansas, though, where her family be. I reckon she'll stay with me as long as I'm walking on God's good earth. Now my boy, he loves it here. Rides his pony around like a little warrior. Says he's 'goin' scoutin' all the time. I told him time and again not to wander out of sight of the cabin, but you know how boys are."

Jake could see that Munsey was a talker. Any questions would be answered with anecdotes and stories. Still, the man might have useful knowledge.

"Been to the Chiricahuas much?" Jake asked after a few moments.

"Some. I used to go to Gayleyville and take food items to the folks out there. Vegetables that we had to spare. Not much, really. Gayleyville was gettin' to be a pretty wild town last I was there. Tombstone's not much better, and it's farther. I made a trek to Tucson once, too. That's a reg'lar city, a'most. This time I went on up to Snowflake. If things get bad again, for whatever reason, I'll take my wife and boy up there to live. Nice country, and I bet there's some good farming."

Jake nodded. "Bet so. Pretty Mormon, though. You a Mormon?"

"I am, sir. I know Mr. Flake personal." Munsey paused for a bit. "I never been to the rocks the Indians talked about. The standing up rocks in the Chiricahuas. Never seen those, but I hear they're quite a sight. A true geologic wonder and a testament to the Lord's creative powers. Heard all the Indians are rounded up out of that area now, but I've seen my share still wanderin' around. Gotta take pity on 'em nowadays. They got no home, nothin' to eat. Real sad what's happened. Real sad. But, they got to learn they can't stand in the way of progress."

Jake remained uncharacteristically quiet and made no comment on Munsey's views, though he had to bite the tip of his tongue to keep from saying anything. "Tell me, Silas, have you ever known any Indians? Personally?"

"I have, indeed. Saw Geronimo once. Met a Navajo this past week -- the one who's carin' for Merriman. Doin' a fine job of it, he is. I'll give him that. Met an Apache recently, too. Called himself Nantan something-or-other."

Jake sat up, suddenly alert. "Nantan Lupan?"

"Yes. I do believe that was it. Scrawny, tough-looking man, but otherwise very agreeable. Leastwise, he left me with my scalp intact."

"When was that?" Jake asked excitedly.

"Well, that was just a bit before I took off for Snowflake, almost a fortnight ago. No, not that long. Eight, no, maybe ten days, perhaps," Munsey said, deep in thought over the length of his journey. "Are you after that man, too?"

"No. Not at all. You might say he's a good friend. Probably the only friend I have, when it comes right down to it. He saved my life." Jake stood and began pacing, now fully energized. "Do you have any idea where he was headed?"

"Nooo…." Munsey paused. "Well, he seemed like a good man, though not a God-fearing one, so I will tell you I believe he was heading into the Chiricahuas. I can give no assurance of that, however."

Jake smiled. Nantan Lupan. Would he still be in the area?

As though reading his mind, Munsey continued, "I hear there's a small group of Apaches that live in the Chiricahuas, still. Maybe three or four. They've avoided the military, and have caused no problems locally that I know of. You might check with a family that now lives in one of the canyons. Erickson is their last name, I believe. The men at the fort can give you directions, I'm sure. Or even perhaps folk in Maley, though I doubt it now that I think about it."

Jake most assuredly wouldn't ask in Maley. Too many people believed that the only good Indian was a dead Indian, and he didn't want to give Nantan Lupan's presence away.

47

"Silas, you've given me the best news I've had in quite a spell. Thank you."

Munsey smiled benevolently. "Well, the Lord works in mysterious ways, Marshal Silver. Mysterious ways." The man continued with his proselytizing until it became plainly clear that Jake would not be a convert. Slowly, he wound down, and soon both men slept. Jake slept more peacefully than he had for some time. For some reason, knowing that Nantan Lupan might still be around gave him a sense of hope and comfort. Nothing escaped Nantan Lupan's knowledge. Somehow, the man would know that he, Jake, was in the area.

While the men slept, Apache and Wild Bill maintained their vigilant watch, stomping occasionally for the hell of it. Munsey's puppy nestled under the man's jacket. The fire slowly died, leaving only a few fading embers.

Far out on the flatland coyotes wailed and outlaws camped. Even farther, a small band of Indians settled deep in a canyon in the Chiricahua Mountains.

INTO THE CHIRICAHUAS

As Jake's journey across the high desert dragged on, his hopes of finding and killing Johnny Geiger ran the gamut from supreme, unalterable confidence to dark despair. That he would find Johnny, he held no doubt. That he would best him in a showdown, however, he often doubted, particularly if the cowardly Geiger had an entourage of outlaws to assist him. For the first time, Jake began to fear dying. Never before had the thought of death aroused trepidation in him. But never before had he anything to lose. Now he had Betsy, and his son…or daughter.

Spurred on by his promise to Betsy to be there for the baby's birth, Jake crossed the intervening miles between him and his nemesis with remarkable rapidity. In short order he arrived in Maley, where the self-appointed mayor directed him to Fort Bowie, a partial day's ride south. There he'd received the most reliable information on the Chiricahuas. Passing through the raucous mining encampment of Dos Cabezas, Jake decided to stop. He recognized the need for rest and sustenance if he wanted to stand any chance in the impending drawdown. "Can't do a good job killing a man if I'm tired and hungry," he told himself. "I want to enjoy every minute of this."

Like many mining towns, unruly miners hurried at all hours of the day to makeshift bars to spend their hard-gotten gold. While liquor flowed freely, soaring spirits and jovial claps on the backs of fellow miners built a false sense of camaraderie. But as surely as night follows day, tempers turned mean as miners' troves of treasure disappeared because of drinking, gambling, and womanizing.

CANYON OF DEATH

Too soon Jake saw his mistake in stopping in the hamlet. Food was not a high priority for the gathered ensemble of soiled doves and dirty earth grubbers, but he managed to get a tough, half-cooked steak in one scroungey establishment. Music of sorts, whooping, and shooting could clearly be heard from one end of the miniscule town to the other, so Jake didn't attempt to find a room in any of the dust-filled hovels somehow standing erect. Irritated and grumpy, he left in search of a quiet enclave in which to sleep.

Off the main road, he found what he sought. A deserted campsite set back in a cleared brushy area afforded him privacy and a modicum of protection. He'd hoped to locate a farmhouse, but he'd seen no habitations other than a few miners' shacks scattered about. The campsite didn't appear to have been used in a while, but still he'd have to maintain some vigilance, even though he planned to cold camp. His horse and mule would help to alert him to passersby, but Jake knew an Apache, or a Mexican for that matter, could sneak up on a tethered animal and charm the hide right off it. Many a traveler had awakened from a deep slumber to find their animals and packs missing. Either the culprit was a "damn Mexican" or a "damn Injun," depending on the person's particular bias. Usually, if they still had their scalps, they blamed the Mexicans. Obviously, though, the thief had to be somebody, and both these groups were known to be deft with animals. So much for a good night's sleep. The odds of finding Geiger first thing were remote at best, so he assured himself that he'd look for a better spot to alight the next day.

Despite his intention of sleeping lightly, Jake awoke in the morning with the sun beginning to lighten the eastern sky, gloriously outlining the Dos Cabezas mountains. The area had obviously gotten its name from the two, dark, rock peaks now being silhouetted by the sun. *The area is so beautiful, it's too bad the inhabitants are so ugly,* he thought. Thankfully, both Apache and Wild Bill stood by patiently, huddling together in the cool morning air.

Invigorated by his good night's rest, Jake packed up quickly. A well-traveled road led directly to the fort, and he arrived in the early afternoon. Pinning his badge on his coat, he was welcomed and quickly found the information and maps he sought.

"These're just hand-drawn, mind you," said the soldier. "But they're damn good. We use 'em all the time."

Jake studied the map before him, which showed a mass of canyons and mountains. "So, the whole area's like this, then? Lots of canyons?"

"Yes, sir."

"Very many people living in the area?"

"A few. Mostly ranchers. There's a small mining town over here called Gayleyville, but it's not much now. A few hangers-on around, maybe. Not a lot of activity going on anymore. Miners up and left."

"How about Indians?"

"Hard to tell about them, sir. Maybe yes. Maybe no. I ain't seen any, myself, but I've heard there's a few out there. They don't seem to be doin' any harm, but we'll get 'em all, sooner or later, don't you worry."

"Any routes you can recommend that're better than others?" Jake asked.

"Not really. The people who know the area best live right here, though." The young man pointed to a canyon at the northern end of the range. "They seem right hospitable. I think their name's Erickson. Can't remember for sure." He paused a moment, deep in thought. "Yeah. That's it. Erickson. Or something like that."

"Thanks," Jake said. "This is a big help."

"You here for any particular reason?"

"You could say that," Jake answered, smiling slightly.

"You after someone?"

Jake merely nodded in response.

"Mind if I ask who?"

"Mind if I ask why you're wanting to know?" Jake asked, leery of letting his intentions go public.

"There was a couple of guys come through here a bit ago. Bad guys. You could tell. Just mean-lookin', bad hombres. They come in with some cattle to sell. After the captain bought 'em we found altered brands on 'em." The youngster leaned over conspiratorially and said in a low voice, "Captain Willard blew his cork. He ain't a man to be fooled with, but we had other matters to attend to and couldn't take off after 'em."

"How many men?" Jake asked.

"Four. Only four rode in, anyway. Got no way of knowin' if there was more waitin' somewhere else."

Four, Jake mused. Well, the odds could be worse, he supposed. He'd handled four men before, but not when Johnny Geiger was one of the four.

"Any chance I can spend the night and get some food before I take off?" Jake asked, never answering the young lieutenant's original question.

"Yes, sir. I'll show you where. Follow me."

The afternoon passed peacefully enough once Jake got the animals fed, watered, and penned. He left some spent shells with the fort's supply officer to get reloaded, and then spent most of the remaining time studying the map he'd been given. He needed a plan. Even if the plan had to be changed, he needed a plan before he could ride out those gates in the morning. A plan gave a man confidence, even if the plan had to be scuttled. Confidence in combat usually predicated the outcome. Usually.

The fort provided lively distraction, reminding him of his time at Fort Huachuca with Peter Burt. He wished Burt would somehow appear. The man's quiet presence and confidence often settled Jake, who had a tendency to be rash and impulsive. Both men shared a steadiness in the line of fire, and steadiness paid rewards – mostly in terms of longevity.

Largely concerned about his upcoming duel, Jake kept to himself at the fort. When spoken to, he responded appropriately, but a reserve about him mostly kept people away. Despite himself, he spent time drawing and target shooting at a small range outside the fort. He didn't have many bullets to spare, but he also didn't have the luxury of not trying to prepare. Accuracy was Jake's real strength with a gun. He was quick enough, but not deadly quick. Still, his accuracy had served him well on most occasions. Geiger, on the other hand, had lightning speed but tended to fire wildly and too early. The man drew so quickly, however, that he'd been known to get off two or three shots before his opponent fired even one. Geiger was somewhat accurate, but nowhere near as accurate as Jake. His weakness lie in his hasty trigger finger. Jake knew this, but he couldn't figure out how the knowledge particularly helped him. His only chance might be to get Geiger rattled, which could make the gunman even more erratic in his aim. But if Geiger traveled with an entourage of cutthroats, there'd be others firing also.

When Jake left the fort the following morning, he knew from that moment forward he had to maintain constant vigilance. Geiger roamed the area. Jake could feel it.

Half a day's ride from the fort brought him to the small ranch the lieutenant had described. Neil and Emma Erickson greeted Jake warmly and made it clear he couldn't leave without, at the very least, partaking a meal with them.

"We don't get many visitors," commented Erickson. "You'd be doing us a favor by staying a bit."

"It'd be my pleasure," Jake said, alighting from his horse.

"You can put your mule and horse up over there," Erickson said, pointing to a small corral. "If they can be hobbled, we've got good grazing out back."

"No one stealing any livestock then?" Jake asked.

"Only once. A week and a half or so ago a small group passed through," Erickson said, a serious look in his eyes. "We noticed a young steer missing right after. Can't say for a fact they rustled the animal. Could've been a cougar, I suppose, but it seems unlikely since we've not had any attacks before or since."

"You're being too easy on those drifters," Jake said as he unsaddled Apache. "If it's the group I think it is, they're up to no good. Guard yourselves and your livestock if you see them slinking around."

"You know these men?"

"You might say so," Jake answered, trying to sound noncommittal.

"You a lawman?" Erickson asked. "I only ask 'cause you got that look about you."

Taking his badge from his pocket, Jake held it out for Erickson to see. Hesitantly, he replied, "Yes, I'm an Arizona Territory U.S. Deputy Marshal. My search for these men, however, is personal more than professional."

"Don't matter none to me, Marshal. Bad men are bad men. Don't matter who kills 'em or why they get killed. They got it coming one way or the other. That's the way I see it. Saw my share of criminals when I served in the military. You got my sympathies and my support," Erickson said. "Now, let's go get a bite to eat."

CANYON OF DEATH

Jake had no doubt the meal Mrs. Erickson served tasted better than anything he could remember eating in the past year. Betsy's nonexistent culinary skills amused him...mostly, although Virginia Hall could cook up a fine feast. Watching the Ericksons interact allowed Jake a dose of nostalgia. The happy couple worked hard, side by side, building their ranch. Jake could plainly see that the couple's dreams for their extensive property brought them great joy. Their small, cozy cabin would one day be an expansive home.

Work on the house resumed shortly after lunch, and if Erickson was surprised that Jake joined in, he showed no sign of it. For Jake's part, helping with the construction gave him reprieve from feelings of doom and the dreary weight of his undertaking. It felt good to work with his hands and to see progress being made before his eyes. Maybe, he pondered as he helped fell a tree, the problem he had with Betsy's ranch was that he felt no sense of ownership. Thomas Jefferson tended to every detail, from riding fence to mending tack and pulling calves. Jake, having been raised on a cattle ranch, knew a considerable amount about livestock, both horses and cattle, but never had he been called upon to put his knowledge to use. *Maybe that's because I'm gone all the time hunting vermin like Geiger,* he thought bitterly as the tree cracked and groaned as though in agony.

Exhausted from a day of manual labor, Jake nevertheless stayed up long enough to question Erickson at length about the area. Erickson examined Jake's map, nodding in approval. "Yah, this is goot," he said, lapsing into a Swedish accent. "Pretty goot." He then showed Jake the best trails across and around the mountains and canyons. "There're many trails. Military makes a lot, but usually they work off old Indian and animal trails."

Remembering Nantan Lupan, Jake asked, "Seen any Apaches in the area?"

"Oh, yah. Plenty times," Erickson answered, pausing a long moment. "I came to this country to avenge my father's death at the hands of Indians. I used to think them heathens. Pure and simple heathens. After some battle engagements and other encounters, however, I found myself having a change of heart. Of course, my thoughts on these matters had to be kept to myself, you understand."

Jake waited patiently while Erickson packed a pipe. He could tell the Swede had more to say on the subject. "No matter what is now said about the matter or claimed to be the truth, the real truth will eventually emerge, which is that the white man drove the Indian from the land and made every effort to completely destroy him. Genocide, Marshal. That's what it would be called in a more civilized country. Not that England, where most of the colonials came from, has ever truly been civilized," he said, a grin now appearing on his face. "Look how the British've treated their own citizens over the years. Horrible. Poor houses. Debtors' prisons. Beggary. No sense of charity in one of 'em. Not a one. No excuse. What else to expect, then, from a growing nation that largely stems from that kind of parentage?"

"Well put, I suppose," Jake said, reluctant to admit the truth of Erickson's simple speech. Although he'd always been a sympathizer to the Native American, Jake had never thought about the causes of the rapaciousness of the American settler.

"I'm fortunate that I found my way to this corner of the world, Marshal. If a few Apaches linger hereabouts, I have no quarrel with that. It is, after all, their land. I've not bought and paid for it. I'd do so gladly, if asked."

"You remember seeing anyone in particular?"

Erickson called out to his wife. "Emma, dear, what's the name of the Indian fellow who's traveled through here a few times? I spoke to him only twice," Erickson said, turning to Jake. "The man speaks Spanish passingly, but not much English. My Spanish is poor at best."

Emma Erickson drew near and sat beside her husband. "I can't remember, dear. But it was like two names. That much I recall. Most of the Indian names I've heard are complicated sounding. This one was short, but definitely sounded like two words."

Jake didn't want to plant a false lead in Emma's mind, but he couldn't refrain from asking, "Was it anything like Nantan Lupan?"

"That might have been it. I really can't say for sure, though. Is he a friend of yours?"

"You could say that."

After a few pleasantries, Emma retired, leaving the two men to continue their discussion. "What do you know about Gayleyville?" Jake asked.

CANYON OF DEATH

"It was faring quite prosperously for a bit, but once miners begin leaving an area, most towns disappear. I fear the same will happen to Gayleyville if it hasn't happened already. It's on the other side of the mountains, you know."

"I see that," Jake said, studying the map again.

"The quickest and easiest route there is right this way," said Erickson, pointing to a trail leading away from his ranch for a ways, then cutting up and over the Chiricahuas. "The nice thing about these mountains is they aren't terribly high, as mountains in the West go. Although, a few peaks come close to the 10,000-foot elevation. There can be snow at these elevations certainly, but usually not until later in the fall. Of course, there's plenty of snowfall in the winter, most winters, anyway. You'll get a chance to see some spectacular rock formations on this route. Unforgettable, really."

"I've heard of them," Jake said.

"The Indians call them 'standing up rocks'." Erickson paused, as if in thought, drawing smoke from his pipe. "I'm really not sure why the Indians had to be run out of this area," he finally said. "Granted, my wife and I will prosper here with them gone, but…" Erickson trailed off.

"Someone recently termed it progress."

Erickson snorted and smiled ruefully. "I suppose," he said, relighting his pipe. "Say, if your friend comes by again, should we tell him you were here?"

"Absolutely. I'd appreciate that. Tell him I'm headed to Gayleyville, if you can manage that in Spanish, anyway. But, I'll tell you, he does speak and understand English pretty well. Just doesn't want to do so."

"I'll figure out a way to make him understand. The fellow seems plenty smart since he's stayed alive and free this long. He'll get my drift, I'm quite certain."

"Give him this," Jake said, taking his badge from his pocket. "Give him this and tell him my name, then say Gayleyville. He'll know."

"But, what if he doesn't come by?"

"Keep the badge, Neil. Give it to your son someday…when you have one. I won't be needing it anymore."

A HOUSEFUL OF WOMEN

Gunner quickly developed a pattern on the ranch. An early riser, he spent mornings checking the fields and animals. Noon meant lunch in the spacious house, and a chance to see Betsy. During the afternoons he worked around the barns and corrals, spending a considerable amount of time every day trying to resettle Betsy's horse, Moonlight.

Betsy remained largely out of sight, although she graced the table occasionally but spoke little. She seemed restive and anxious. Perhaps that's how expectant ladies got, Gunner mused. Or perhaps as her time drew near she worried that Jake would not return as he'd promised, which Gunner thought more likely the cause of her mood.

One afternoon he reluctantly escorted Betsy to Thomas Jefferson's gravesite when asked to do so. He wondered if the long stroll in the cool air would be harmful for her, and worried that seeing the man's grave might cause her undue emotional stress. The second count proved correct.

He stood aside as Betsy paid her respects to the fallen ranch hand. Then, like a wounded, abandoned child, he watched her slump to the ground and sob. Uncertain whether to leave her to cry alone or to offer comfort, he stood awkwardly for a moment, until she stretched her hand in his direction.

He knelt beside the weeping girl, afraid to touch her, yet intuitively understanding that a tender, sympathetic touch was what she most craved. Carefully, he placed his hand on her shoulder and gently squeezed it. He remained silent, not sure what to say, fearing he'd say the wrong thing.

"He was so good to me," Betsy sobbed, her tear-streaked face looking more sad than he could ever have imagined.

"I loved him. He took good care of me and this place. Always smiling. Never complained. Not once. So kind. Gentle." Her voice shook as weeping choked the words.

"Yes, ma'am," Gunner mumbled, not knowing what else to say.

"It's just not fair that he had to die! Why? Why, Gunner? It's not fair!" And she flung herself fully onto the ground.

Gunner finally sprang into action. "Betsy, you can't lie on the ground like this. It's cold. You've got the baby to think of," he said as he gently pulled her to her feet.

"Why do you care so much about this baby, Gunner?" she asked, facing him confrontationally, her voice raising.

Gunner stood silent, embarrassed, not certain what to say.

"I want an answer!" she demanded. "Why? Why do you care? The father sure as hell doesn't care."

Surprising himself, Gunner began a half-hearted defense of Jake. "I'm sure he cares very much, Betsy. But he's got to make things right."

"He needs to be here with me, Gunner."

"And I'm sure he'd like to be, but...." Gunner paused, stiffening. "We need to get you back to the house, Betsy. No more of this talk."

He led the silent girl back, angry that he'd defended Jake. Angry that he wasn't the man she loved. Angry with her for loving the wrong man. Angry about everything.

"You wouldn't have left me, Gunner, if you were the father, would you? I know you wouldn't have."

"I'm *not* the father, Betsy. No sense talking this foolishness. You're upset. I won't hear any more of it." He opened the front door. Both entered and stopped abruptly, surprised by the presence of strangers in the drawing room. The woman looked vaguely familiar, yet neither could place where they'd seen her before. A tall man in uniform stood by her side. Virginia Hall rose from the settee, smiling, but no one spoke for a moment.

"Betsy?" the woman asked, stepping forward.

"Yes."

"Betsy, it's so good to meet you. I'm Sophy, Jake's sister. Jake has told me so much about you."

A long moment passed before anyone spoke. Suddenly, it became clear why the woman looked so familiar, and Betsy's anger at Jake instantly melted. "Sophy! Sophy, I've heard so much about you!" Betsy said as the two women gently hugged each other. "But, what are you doing here? How...?" Questions formed too rapidly, and Betsy looked adoringly at the woman before her. "Have you met Virginia? She's been staying with me until Jake...oh, Jake is looking for a man who kidnapped me. Did you know that? Oh my. I've got hundreds of questions for you! How'd you know where I lived? How'd you get here?"

Gunner could see his services were no longer needed and began backing away. "Wait! Betsy said, "You must stay, Gunner. This is Jake's sister, Sophy. And you are?" Betsy asked, looking to the military man.

"Captain Peter Burt, at your service," he said, smiling warmly at the excited and clearly expectant girl. "I escorted Miz Silver here from Fort Huachuca. I'm a friend of Jake's. I've been transferred to the fort here. I'll take my leave now and let you two ladies get acquainted."

"Oh, no! You must stay. I'm sure Virginia will prepare a meal for all of us, won't you Virginia?" Betsy turned to her companion.

"On another occasion perhaps, Miss – " Burt hesitated, obviously uncertain how to address Betsy. "I do have to report to the fort immediately, and I know the journey has left Miz Silver fatigued."

"Of course. Of course," Betsy said, flushed with excitement. "It's a pleasure to meet you, Captain Burt. Please, come by any time."

Gunner found the moment convenient to exit also. Outside, he felt Captain Burt examining him closely.

"I hear good things about you from Miss Hall," Burt finally said. "I'm sure Jake will appreciate your staying on and taking care of things until he returns."

Gunner nodded, uncertain how to reply. Had he just received an order to leave the moment Jake returned?

"When did you last see Jake?" Burt asked.

"Right before I left for Freeman with Betsy. He was leaving to go after an outlaw named Johnny Geiger."

"By himself?"

"I suppose. Wasn't anybody around willing to go with him."

"Any idea where he headed?"

"I heard tell that Geiger'd run off down into the Chiricahua area," Gunner replied. "Haven't heard anything since then."

Burt stood silent a moment, then turned to descend the porch steps. "I'll be at the fort. Let me know if there's anything, anything at all, that goes awry around here."

Gunner nodded again. He stood a moment watching Burt mount and ride down the entry lane. He contemplated whether to go back and scrounge some food in the kitchen, or wait until Virginia rang the triangle dinner bell. Would Virginia stay on now that Jake's sister had arrived? Probably not. She had a boarding house to run. He hoped Sophy would be as good a cook as Virginia'd been. Who was going to deliver the baby if Virginia left? Jake's sister didn't look to be the baby-delivering type.

Ambling to the corral, he wondered what had gotten into Betsy earlier at the gravesite. She'd talked like she stood ready to wash her hands of Jake, but when his sister'd arrived, she became all aflutter with excitement, carrying on as though sending Jake packing would be the farthest thing from her mind. Like she couldn't be happier. Such unpredictability and emotional displays struck him as odd, but his experience with the fair sex up till now had never been more than fleeting. Obviously, the women he knew made their livelihoods being funny, loving, and sweet. Except, of course, for his mother. He felt vaguely perplexed and uncomfortable about all of it.

Dinner that evening began as a festive affair. Apparently, both women had spent the day resting, for they both appeared cheerful and good-humored at the table. Despite Gunner suggesting that he take his meal in the kitchen so the ladies could talk more freely, no one would hear of it. Conversation began airily enough, but as the meal proceeded, Gunner spotted impending trouble, particularly once the conversation turned to Jake.

"I didn't know you and Jake had married," Sophy remarked innocently. "That's just like him though. Not to tell me anything until after the fact," she said, smiling.

The silence that hung in the air made Gunner squirm uncomfortably. He looked quickly down at his plate, but couldn't stop himself from casting a furtive glance in Betsy's direction. Oh, no. Tears again.

"Well, we're not exactly married. Jake has asked me to marry him, but I…I haven't decided," Betsy finally said, a note of triumph detectable in her voice.

No one spoke for a brief spell, uncertain where to take the conversation next.

"Well, if you'll all just excuse me, I believe I'd best retire to do some harness work down in the barn," Gunner commented. "Mighty fine dinner, Miss Hall. As always." Gunner stood, awkwardly avoiding eye contact with anyone.

"Nonsense, Gunner. Please be seated," Betsy said assertively. "We haven't had dessert, and I know Virginia has made a chocolate cake for this occasion."

Gunner hesitated, uncertain whether to acquiesce to Betsy's request and help her save face, or ignore her and save his own. "Well, I thank you, Betsy, but I'm thinking I'll hold off on that dessert for a spell. You all have a nice evening."

Before she could respond, he left the table and strode purposefully from the room.

On the porch, he breathed a sigh of relief. Things were just getting too uncomfortable for him in the house. He'd have to show up after mealtimes so he could eat alone. At this point, why any man would want to settle down with a woman when, from his experience, they seemed to be mostly unpredictable, emotional, and incapable of carrying their own weight, baffled him. Maybe that's why Jake'd taken off after Geiger. Maybe the problem wasn't Geiger, maybe Jake just didn't want to be tied down to all this fussing and carrying on and woman stuff. Still, when he thought of Betsy's bright blue eyes, her beautiful smile, and womanly attraction, he felt a stirring deep within himself. Confused, he continued to the barn.

Darkness kept him from trying to halter Moonlight and working with the animal. It had been a mystery to him, why a horse that had carried Betsy safely several hundred miles had become so unmanageable. He'd heard of horses reverting to the wild for no apparent reason, and maybe this was the case with this animal. Although, he thought that most any horse that reverted to a feral state most likely did so from a cause. He doubted that the horse had ingested loco weed. Possibly it could have been mistreated or beaten these past weeks, but he doubted that also. He'd heard of other maladies, strange and unusual ones such as rabies afflicting horses. Baffled, he watched the animal eat and noticed the horse remained wary of him the whole time, stomping nervously, the whites of its eyes showing. Neglect might cause a horse to revert to unacceptable behavior, at least for a spell, but Moonlight'd been back on the ranch for a while now. Even after making a point to try to handle the horse several times a day, every day, he'd seen little change in the animal. He'd not yet tried to saddle and mount him. Maybe he'd leave that for Jake Silver. He smirked as he pictured Jake thrown on his ass.

Gunner wandered into the small but comfortable room that had been Thomas Jefferson's. The ranch hand's few clothing articles had been folded and placed with care in a small bureau. Gunner'd felt awkward removing the man's possessions, so he hadn't touched anything, and kept his own clothes in a pile on the floor. Not that he had many clothes. Some of the shirts and pants he found himself forced to wear when his were being laundered by the meticulous Miss Hall were obviously Jake's.

Gunner stretched out, fully clothed, on Jefferson's cot. He now regretted his agreement to stay on the premises until Jake returned. Hells fire. That could be months, he suddenly realized. But he couldn't imagine how the two, now three, women would manage without some kind of assistance. None of the three looked to be physically up to the work the ranch demanded. Miss Hall was well beyond the age of toting hay and handling livestock. And even if Betsy weren't expecting, both she and Sophy were too slight – although he'd seen his own mother, a diminutive woman herself, handle chores one would expect from a full-grown man. Still, this situation seemed different. The thought that Betsy could hire someone from town never entered his mind.

The clanging triangle bell raised Gunner from his reverie. What the hell? Realizing something unexpected must have happened, he quickly arose. Emerging from the barn, he broke into a dead run when he heard Virginia's frantic voice calling for him.

"Betsy's time has come. Run get the doctor, quick as you can. I fear there may be trouble. Hurry, Gunner!"

"Yes, ma'am," Gunner replied, his heart suddenly thumping wildly.

The mad ride to town passed in both a blur and in slow motion. He couldn't remember a thing, except that it seemed like it took him forever to race wildly down the dark lane to Prescott. The return seemed a torturous trip from hell as the horse drawing the doctor's conveyance never went faster than a trot.

"Doc, you gotta hurry," Gunner repeated several times.

"It does me no good to get there, son, if I'm dead upon arrival," the doctor replied the first time. After that, he ignored Gunner's urgings and drove steadily on, commenting once that he'd rarely seen a young man so anxious about the birth of a child. After that, Gunner remained silent.

Hours after being sent on his mission, Gunner and the doctor entered the house to hear Betsy's piercing screams. "Good, it sounds as though things are well underway," the physician commented as he mounted the steps. Turning to Gunner, who hung back, nervously turning his hat in his hands, he directed, "Go boil a big pot of water, young man."

"You're too late, doctor," Virginia Hall spoke from the landing at the top of the stairway.

Gunner awoke on the floor with Sophy administering smelling salts.

THE WIND WHISPERED

From high on a ridge, hidden between two large pillars of stone, Nantan Lupan watched the rider as he wound around large rocky outcroppings. The Indian cracked the smallest of grins. Different from other white men, the man who now advanced had a connection with Nantan Lupan like no other. No other white deserved to live, and maybe not even this man deserved to do so, but Nantan Lupan regarded Jake Silver with a sense of camaraderie and respect.

Nantan Lupan had been expecting the rider. He'd watched for him for several days, and today he would return to his camp with his friend. He had information for him. Warnings. News of the small band of deadly men and renegades who waited with evil in mind. Well, there was one less renegade now. Several days ago, he had not hesitated to kill one of the Navajos who rode with the outlaws. The Indian held a Navajo girl in bondage, and when the man headed into the brush to have his way with the girl, to much laughter and jeering from the others, his abuse of the young woman turned Nantan Lupan's stomach, a most rare experience. He wondered if his abhorrence of the Navaho's treatment of the girl signified that he was growing older and weaker in mind and spirit. But the girl's pitiful screams brought back memories of his Sophee, and Nantan Lupan responded rashly, rushing the much larger Navajo, taking him by surprise and slitting his throat. He'd not violated the man, something he would not have hesitated to do to a white man, although he'd looked into the dying renegade's eyes and spat upon him.

The girl quaked in fear and doubled her small fists to defend herself against Nantan Lupan. He ignored her defensive posturing and signaled for her to join him. He cared not whether she accepted his invitation, but he suspected she would. Both knew she would not last long once the white men came looking for her and the Navajo when the two didn't show up. Slowly, she unfurled her fists and followed him to his mount. Neither spoke as he pulled her up behind him.

Neither had yet spoken, even though they'd been encamped together for several days. Nantan Lupan approached the girl the first evening he'd brought her to the camp, and she'd willingly accepted him – most likely out of gratitude, but he didn't care. He'd not held a woman in many moons, and visions of Sophee teased him throughout his coupling with the girl. Since that evening, the girl followed him like a faithful puppy, fearful when he left her in camp alone, and joyful when he returned. Even yet, neither spoke, but words had not been necessary. What would he say, even if he spoke her tongue? If she remained with him, he would treat her well and take her with him to Sonora. If she left, he would find a Mexican girl to serve his needs. It felt good, though, to have a woman. One Jake Silver would not take from him, as the man had Sophee.

Nantan Lupan watched Jake's slow, cautious progress. The marshal did not ride in hot pursuit, but rather traveled as if contemplating a best course of action. He rode warily, looking for tracks and signs of riders, approaching areas of likely ambush with weaponry drawn. Nantan Lupan puzzled over what had caused the man to revert from wildly bold and aggressive to cautious. The marshal pursued a nasty, vicious bunch, and the Apache admired Jake's vigilance, prudence, and wisdom. Qualities he'd not seen in his friend before now.

Nantan Lupan knew precisely where the outlaws camped, which was a distance away, so he turned his pony and began working down the steep, rocky switchback. He'd meet the marshal en route.

***

Jake Silver felt watched. No matter how carefully he scanned the hillsides and surrounding terrain, he had the uncanny feeling that someone observed him. Expecting the report of a bullet any moment, he rode cautiously, ready to bail from his mount and roll behind any nearby colossal boulder for protection. Once he thought he'd seen movement on high between two "standing up rocks," large pillars of stone with a crevice between them. From a distance the crevice appeared miniscule, but Jake figured the opening to be much larger than it looked – large enough to hide a mounted rider.

He'd reluctantly left the Erickson homestead at dawn. His thoughts might be nothing but flights of fancy, but he wondered, if he'd stayed on if Nantan Lupan might, by some stroke of magnificent luck, have wandered by the homestead again. The Indian's presence would be a great boon to Jake's flagging spirits. Between pondering how best to take the men out, dwelling on Johnny Geiger's lightning-fast draw, and watching for signs of the desperadoes, he found himself strung to fiddle-string tightness and wondered how long he could maintain this level of alertness. After a few hours of strained concentration, his attention wandered. His gaze drank in the magnificent rock formations and no longer focused on possible sites of ambush. *What the hell. It's a beautiful place to die. I gotta give it that,* he thought as the morning sun finally broke over the top of the mountain before him, warming him slowly. He'd stop up ahead and remove his mackinaw and give the animals a rest. He wondered if this might be a good place to leave the mule tethered. Leading the animal along the narrow trail had already become increasingly troublesome and would slow him down considerably if the route narrowed much more, which it seemed likely to do. No sooner had the thought entered his mind, however, than he felt reluctant to leave Wild Bill behind. Certainly, he couldn't be becoming attached to the wooly, large-eared creature. He shouldn't have let Ben McGraw talk him into bringing him, but he had to admit the additional blankets and supplies had been right useful.

Coming to a flat, well-treed area, Jake dismounted and allowed the animals to forage on the clumps of native grasses. After tethering both animals, he removed a sack filled with Mrs. Erickson's homemade delights from his saddlebag, and then he saw him. A slow smile spread across Jake's face as Nantan Lupan nodded in response.

"About time you showed up," Jake said, relief swamping him.

"'Bout time *you* showed up," the Indian responded. "I wait for you many days."

CANYON OF DEATH

"How'd you know I was even coming?" Jake asked, curious about the source of the Indian's information. If Nantan Lupan knew he'd show up, maybe the desperadoes he hunted also knew. He figured they did, but hoped they didn't.

Nantan Lupan smiled slowly. "I heard the wind whisper your name," he replied softly, dismounting and walking toward Jake.

The two men, former enemies, clasped arms in friendship. "I'm glad to see you, Nantan Lupan. You're a welcome sight for sorry eyes, I gotta admit."

The Indian nodded. "You will use my help in days to come."

So, he knew. It puzzled Jake how the Indian had come about his knowledge, but Indians had ways of communicating that whites didn't understand. Sometimes runners made their way from village to village spreading rumors and gossip. More often, Jake figured keen observation gave them most of the information they needed.

"Have you seen them?" he asked.

"There rode seven. Now only six."

"Thank you. That narrows the odds a bit," Jake said, smiling and showing a nonchalance he didn't feel. "Are they far?"

"Yes. They move to end of mountains. Canyon close to Mexico. Two days from here."

"Guess I better change direction, then. Lost their tracks a ways back. I was wondering if they changed direction when they crossed that flat, stony area."

"Come to my encampment. We talk. Eat. Plan," Nantan Lupan said. "These men take much planning."

"I think I'll do just that," Jake responded. Although he wanted to continue the pursuit, his need of the Indian's companionship outweighed all else. Already he felt stronger, and wiser, with Nantan Lupan present. The wily Indian's advice could not be disregarded. He alone out of Geronimo's once fierce tribe survived as a free man, roaming his corner of the world at will despite the military's continuous manhunt. Judging by the maps he'd gotten at Fort Bowie, Jake knew soldiers regularly crisscrossed these mountains, yet Nantan Lupan lived in impunity beneath their very noses.

"Is it far?"

"Never far to a man's camp where food and fire await," Nantan Lupan answered.

Jake shrugged. What the hell. If nothing else, the detour would delay the inevitable.

The trek to Nantan Lupan's encampment took longer than Jake expected, especially with Wild Bill balking much of the way. Referring to Wild Bill as a long-eared devil, Nantan Lupan looked with disgust upon the furry critter, but more than once Jake caught the Indian stealing admiring glances at his horse, Apache.

"Named this horse after you," Jake said. "I call him Apache."

Nantan Lupan smiled crafily. "Perhaps he will then welcome me as a new master?"

"Don't count on it. Besides, you'll have your choice of horses once we gun down the outlaws."

"No one ride a horse like yours. I trade you my woman for your horse," Nantan Lupan teased.

Jake smiled in response to the Indian's suggestion.

The surprise was Jake's, however, when an Indian girl rushed to meet the two riders as they entered camp. The girl anxiously grabbed onto Nantan Lupan, fearful of the white man accompanying him.

"Where'd you get the girl?" Jake asked.

"From Navajo I killed."

"I think she's the one that was stolen up north."

Nantan Lupan did not respond to Jake's statement, but stoked the fire and handed the girl a freshly killed rabbit and partridge, which she skillfully set about skinning and plucking.

The Indian's camp lie hidden in an almost impenetrable thicket of shrubs, surrounded by a dense grove of young pines and oak. A narrow trail, well hidden by loose branches that Nantan Lupan had removed and then replaced behind them, led to a small, cleared area in front of a rocky outcropping which provided protection from the elements. By anyone's standards, it was a hell of an encampment.

The sun had already crept past its zenith, and Jake welcomed the brief heat of the fall afternoon. It would grow quite cold tonight at this altitude, and again he was glad for the extra blankets Ben McGraw had insisted he take. He'd leave the bundle with Nantan Lupan and his woman when he left.

The two men sat in the open, absorbing the heat of the sun in the tranquil afternoon.

"Snow come soon. I go Sonora," Nantan Lupan said.

"I thought you'd already be in Mexico. What held you up?"

"Hmmph. You lucky man I still here," the Indian replied.

"You taking your woman?" Jake asked, wondering if he'd be returning her to her tribe.

"If woman follow."

Jake nodded in response. It wasn't like Nantan Lupan to be so noncommittal. He certainly hadn't been when it came to Sophy. Perhaps he hid his feelings. He wondered why Indians insisted on being so stoic. *But you never do that, do you?* flitted through his head.

The two lolled about while the girl busied herself continuously, always keeping a wary eye on Jake. "How'd you come across her?" Jake asked.

"I say already. One less man for you to kill," Nantan Lupan answered.

All afternoon Jake pondered the best way to take the men out. A shootout would not be feasible lest his ammunition run out. He'd hoarded his bullets, not shooting at anything unless guaranteed a sure shot, but still, he didn't know how much fire power the enemy had. Best to pick them off, if possible. Nantan Lupan would be indispensible in this matter, but Jake began to harbor some reluctance about using and endangering the man.

"I'll leave in the morning," Jake said after several hours of silence.

"Rain in the new day. Big wind. No go tomorrow."

Jake looked above and saw nothing but azure, although he noted a growing pallor when he studied the sky. He'd wait and see.

After dinner, as the men sat by the fire, Nantan Lupan spoke. "My time here is over. White men move into meadows where deer and antelope once ranged. No grass remains. White man churns the earth to plant seeds. White man's cattle eat what grass is left." He paused for a minute before resuming. "Animals leave the area. I leave. Never to return. This will be our last meeting, my friend."

"You can come to Prescott when I go back. You can stay with me. Be a scout. I'll protect you," Jake offered.

"No man take care of me. I am not a woman."

Jake nodded in understanding. He'd grown fond of the Indian, and the thought of losing what seemed like his only friend bothered him. "My offer stands. Always you will be welcome," he added.

Nantan Lupan did not respond, but began humming a sad melody. It wouldn't matter anyway if the upcoming battle went as Jake feared. Still, he had to face Johnny Geiger, no matter the outcome. Perhaps his hatred for Johnny would even things up.

As Nantan Lupan continued his mournful chant, Jake's thoughts turned to Betsy. He'd gone out of his way to avoid thinking of her, often abruptly shutting her out when his mind wandered and she flitted into his head. He wondered how she fared. He refused to remember her downcast face the morning he sent her to Freeman with Gunner McGraw. Sighing, he wondered if she'd ever understand that he had to get Johnny Geiger. If he were honest, it wasn't just Betsy he had to avenge, but the direct challenge to himself. Johnny had thrown down the gauntlet. Ego had nothing to do with it, he told himself.

He'd lost count of the days on the trail, but he figured he'd been traveling maybe three weeks, give or take. In another few days the ordeal would be over, one way or another. If his luck held, he'd be heading back before any serious snow flew. If he could avoid any heavy weather he'd have been gone and back in two months or so. He'd promised Betsy he'd be home for the baby's birth, and he would be, although he'd have to travel to Freeman where Gunner had taken her. He'd leave the mule off with Ben McGraw. Save him a trip otherwise.

Nantan Lupan's woman smiled appreciatively when Jake removed heavy, woolen blankets from the mule's pack for them. "Yours," he said. The girl looked fully at him and smiled for the first time. A strikingly pretty girl, she would make Nantan Lupan happy. He had no doubt the girl would follow the Indian to the ends of the earth if needed. Would Betsy do so with him? He shook his head at the answer. Why would she? She had everything she needed and wanted. Jake could offer her only love and bodily comfort, but so could any man, and even that now caused her trouble and shame. Quickly, he shut her from his mind. He'd be better off spending his time planning the upcoming gunfight.

CANYON OF DEATH

Nantan Lupan unexpectedly spoke, breaking Jake's reverie. "Tomorrow we plan. Gather food. Wait for storm to pass. We leave with the next sun."

"I don't want you to go, Nantan Lupan. You could get killed. You have a woman now who needs you."

"Bah! Speak no more of this. I go," the Indian retorted, turning abruptly and striding to the covered embankment where he and the girl slept.

Jake smiled. Damn stubborn fool. Still, he felt relieved knowing that he had someone as fearsome as Nantan Lupan to watch his back. He couldn't ask for better. He'd repay the Indian somehow, but Lord only knew he didn't want to have to owe the man yet again for his life. He remembered the other shootout. The Apache had unexpectedly appeared during the fray to save his skin when Jake had been en route home after wresting his sister, Sophy, from him. No, he held no doubt that Nantan Lupan had saved his life on that occasion.

Jake stretched out by the fire and watched Apache and Wild Bill doze. He'd move under the ledge with the others if it started to rain, which he doubted it would. Several hours later, however, he awoke to the splatter of cold raindrops on his face. How the heck could that Indian always know what the weather was going to do?

The next day it rained heavily, and the three sat bundled up under the protection of the overhanging rock ledge. Although antsy to move on, resting felt good to Jake. The girl brought fire into the cave-like ledge, and once the rocks absorbed heat from the flames it felt almost warm.

By early afternoon the rain began to subside, and Nantan Lupan went out in search of game. He returned empty-handed several hours later. "Animals go. Snow coming."

Jake retrieved the stores of dried food McGraw had sent along from the mule's pack and shared it with the couple. He hadn't eaten much of it because hunting had been darn good up until then.

Nantan Lupan, normally taciturn, talked that night until the fire burned down to embers. He told stories of Geronimo, Victorio, the giant Mangus Colorado, and other great Apache chiefs and their astounding bravery and feats. Geronimo he'd known personally, but most of the others he'd learned of from elders telling tales around the campfire. Jake asked a lot of questions, hoping to glean a war tactic he could use on the outlaws he'd soon have to face. The main point of many of the stories seemed to be that the Apaches had achieved victory on most occasions despite being vastly outnumbered. The tales encouraged Jake, who often faced great odds himself when he challenged a criminal. Few criminals rode alone. Most always had sidekicks who were as bad or worse. His upcoming confrontation seemed doable, except for the fact that he just had a bad, bad feeling about it.

OUTLAW

"He ain't comin', Johnny. What we wastin' our damn fool time for hangin' around this country? Let's move on. It's gettin' cold, too," Red Langley whined.

"Don't you worry your puny little brain none," Johnny Geiger responded, flicking a cigarette into the fire. "He's a'comin'. I can smell 'im,"

The other four outlaws remained silent, watching the drama they'd been anticipating unfold. Red Langley had drawn the short straw that morning, and it remained up to him to talk some sense into crazy Johnny.

"Whyn't we just mosey on down to Mexico for a coupla days and get us some women and tequila?" Red continued. "This ain't no life sittin' here watchin' the wind blow, Johnny. We oughtta be havin' us some fun. We got that money from the soldier boys for them cattle we rustled. Let's do a little livin'."

"Shut your trap, Red, before I shut it for ya. We ain't leavin' this place until the mighty U.S. Deputy Marshal Jake Silver lies dead in it. And wipe that damn tobacco juice off'n yer chin," Johnny retorted.

Red dutifully ran his hand over his grizzled chin, then wiped it on the leg of his pants. He looked remorsefully at his companions, who shook their heads in disgust at his failure. Angered by their response, Red said, "Well, you all can just stay put, then. I'm headin' on down to Mexico way and have me some fun." He stood, clearly uncertain what to do or say next.

"Bye. Have fun." Johnny's eyes narrowed as he spoke.

"I just need me a little of that money we got for those longhorn. Jus' what's rightly my share," Red said.

CANYON OF DEATH

"You get nothin' till the job's done. That's the deal. You don't like it, you walk. 'Course, it's gonna be difficult to do that when you got a bullet in your butt," Johnny said, to the amusement of the other desperadoes.

Red sat back down. "Now I never said I was goin' right this minute, Johnny. An' I don't like you threat'nin' me none, neither."

Geiger shook his head in disgust, stood and strolled away, chewing on a piece of dry grass. He knew restlessness to be a contagious fever among men, but he didn't know what to do about it. Maybe the men were more liability than help and he should just get rid of 'em now. The idea appealed to him, but he hesitated. That damn Jake Silver was one lucky, sly fox. Though he resisted admitting it, deep down Geiger feared he might need help putting away the lawman. His lightning-quick draw remained the fastest yet, but Silver was deadly accurate, especially with a rifle. If the man got off a shot, Geiger knew it'd probably be over for him. But one of 'em had to go, as far as Geiger was concerned. Shoulda happened years ago.

The five men accompanying Geiger had been a weight on him since they'd gotten to this canyon, where Johnny had determined the final showdown with Jake Silver would take place. The setup was perfect. The canyon, more of a valley, ran between sloping bluffs. He could strategically position men along the hillsides. Behind them, the steep canyon head would prevent anyone from approaching from that direction. There was, in Johnny's mind, only one way in and one way out. He'd know when Silver approached and he'd be ready. He'd told the others repeatedly that no one was to shoot Silver but him. They could shoot the hell out of anyone foolish enough to accompany Silver, but the marshal belonged to Johnny alone.

If pressed, Johnny could not explain the great enmity he felt for his childhood nemesis. "I hate that sumbitch," he often said while drunk. And every time he said it, he realized it was the only truth he knew. His whole life Silver had bested him at everything. Silver was better looking, bigger, stronger, a better shot, fearless, tougher, smarter. The list went on. What probably rubbed him the rawest was Jake's good looks and the way the female sex always pandered to him. He'd been left with Jake's seconds his whole life.

Johnny knew he'd gone too far, though, with the little blonde up in Prescott. Mouthy little snot. He'd sure as hell knocked some sense into her.

He didn't mind pushing women around. It amused him that they were so defenseless and soft. Disgusted him, really. But Jake's woman – she deserved what she got. He mostly hit women with an open hand, or at most the heel of his hand, but her, he'd finally doubled his fist and belted her a couple good ones. She didn't know when to shut the hell up. If she'd just shut her trap he wouldn't have beat her so bad. But no, she had to taunt him, call him names, tell him that Jake'd get him good for what he was doin' to her. He wanted to beat her to death, but he stopped just short. Then he discovered she was preggers, so he just left her in the desert to let nature take its course. Her pregnancy repulsed him. Not sure why. So, he left her where she dropped. Good riddance to that mouthy piece of baggage. Desert did her in, he felt sure.

But it was all for the good. Now Silver would come barreling headlong in for revenge. Johnny snickered. Whee! This was gonna be too good to be true. He knew Silver was coming. The trader had told them. When pressed, various people along the way recalled seeing the lone rider. And Johnny knew Jake Silver, and he knew Jake would not let this assault go unpunished. Pride. Yeah, Jake had more pride – and a bigger temper, too.

"Red, since you got nothin' better to do than let your mouth run away with itself, you go relieve that Navajo on watch. And keep your eyes open! The next time I catch you sleepin' on watch, you'll never open yer damn eyes again. Understand?" Johnny knew Red wouldn't argue much, and he knew damn well that Red understood he'd already pushed too far.

Red started to argue, but relented. Standing, he snatched his hat off the ground and mounted his horse. He turned to say something but hesitated. Instead, he did as bid.

"Don't see how you put up with that nitwit, Johnny," Smithy said. "He's always tryin' to stir trouble up about somethin'."

Johnny surmised that Smithy was as much to blame for Red's earlier outburst as Red himself. Probably put Red up to it, in fact. Wanted Red's share of the money, that was all.

"Johnny? You sure he's comin?" Boots asked. "I don't doubt you none, but what makes you so certain Silver's comin'?"

"I know the man better'n I know myself. He's predictable, gentlemen. He'll come. It's the right thing to do, and if there's one thing you can count on, it's that Marshal Jake Silver prides himself on doin' the right thing. He'll show. I beat on his woman. He won't let that go. Not on your life." Johnny paused a moment. "Now none of you boys better start jawin' on me about this. I've had a bellyful as it is. He's comin'. I can feel it. I know the man. You got nothin' better to do anyway 'cept run from the law. So shut the hell up."

Neither Smithy nor Boots nor the two new recruits Johnny'd picked up in Dos Cabezas responded. The new members of the group claimed Silver had shot two of their partners in the mountain passes, and they wanted revenge.

Johnny's speed with a gun was legendary. Even if all of them drew down on him at once, probably three of them would lie dead within a split second. And there were no guarantees who the lone survivor might be.

After a few moments, Boots spoke up again. "You got a plan, Johnny? Might be a good time to tell us what you 'spect so's we know our jobs if you're really thinkin' he's headin' this way right now."

"I told you before, you dumb ass. You shoot anyone with him you want, but you don't shoot him unless by some crazy stroke of luck he guns me down. Then you pump him so full of lead he rusts before the animals scavenge him." Exasperated, Johnny continued, "How many more times I gotta tell you the same damn thing? It ain't no plan. It's a slaughter."

Boots nodded, smiling. "Just checkin', boss."

Johnny sighed. It would be another long day. Maybe he should go in pursuit of Silver. No. If Silver hadn't arrived in two days, then he'd rethink things. He just wished he had that Navajo girl they'd taken from up north right now. He could use a woman to pass the time of day, even if she was Indian. It'd do all the boys some good, come right down to it. He wondered what the hell had become of her. Red and Boots had gone back to find the missing pair when they'd not shown up that afternoon. They found the man with his throat slit, but the girl was nowhere in sight. Could that little thing have slit the brave's throat? Johnny smiled at the thought. He could use a little spitfire like that. She'd be able to withstand a lot of beating. Just like Jake's blonde girlfriend.

He heard Red approaching, the horse's hooves thundering up the canyon. "Johnny!" Red panted heavily. "The Indian's gone. He's not where he's s'post to be. He done took off."

Johnny thought the matter over a minute. "You sure he just wasn't off in the bushes doin' his job?"

"He's gone. Not one trace of 'im."

"No loss. I didn't trust that redskin anyway. Never understood why those two Indians wanted to join up with us. My scalp feels better already," Johnny said in an effort to make light of the situation. The Indian had been a cold-blooded killer, willing to torture and kill anyone Johnny gave him the go-ahead to do so, but he was also a superb scout who thoroughly knew the area. Johnny doubted the man had taken off. More than likely he was scoutin' around.

"Well, that just means one less hungry gut to fill. No loss, boys. Buck up."

"Just means more money for each of us," Boots said, nodding happily.

"More money for me, you mean," Johnny snapped, leaving no one with the false impression the Indian's share of the loot would be distributed among them. "Get back on watch, Red. Boots will relieve you tonight. The rest of you will have to divide up the watch time. It won't be for long, though."

***

The tortuous climb made Jake's legs burn. They'd left the two horses at the base of the mountain, the trek too steep for the animals, and way too steep for Jake, too, as far as he was concerned.

It'd been Nantan Lupan's plan to climb over the top of the mountain. The outlaws, he'd argued, would not expect them to approach from that direction. They'd be watching the canyon entrance. It'd made perfect sense to Jake, until he saw the mountain they'd be scaling. Even then it seemed doable, but now that his legs felt on fire and thousands of feet separated him from the base of the mountain, he second guessed the decision.

Nantan Lupan clambered up the rocks like a mountain goat, surefooted and quickly. Jake kept the Indian's pace for a distance, but as they neared the top he lagged. "Can't let that little bugger outdo me on this," he muttered. They missed the snowline by cutting across a lower crag, but the freezing air kept Jake moving lest his sweat-soaked clothing cooled and gave him hypothermia. He'd left his coat tied to the back of the saddle far below. He hoped they wouldn't have to return this same route.

Nantan Lupan remained certain that the murderous gang awaited in that particular canyon. "Men in canyon – canyon of death," he'd repeated when Jake questioned his source of information.

The two men had been climbing and scampering about on rocky cliffs for the better part of the morning, when suddenly Nantan Lupan began to urge Jake on. "We must reach top while sun still rising. Sun blind men below to our presence. Not much farther."

Jake renewed his efforts, and in half an hour they reached the summit. At first the canyon seemed deserted, but after a few minutes of carefully scanning the area, Nantan Lupan detected movement. The Indian prided himself on his keen eyesight and pointed out the five men to Jake. Only after the Apache had done so, did Jake readily see them in the canyon far below. Jake had heard there were two outlaws and two renegades riding with Johnny. He'd felt better when he'd learned that Nantan Lupan had taken one of the renegades out. But now, he saw two more outlaws accompanying Johnny than he'd figured on.

"Okay. What now?" Jake deferred to the Indian and his knowledge of the area.

"Animals walk on trail down the canyon wall. Move fast but with care. Do not let feet make rocks fall."

Gulping water from his canteen, Jake nodded.

"Me first. You follow. No talk."

The two began edging down the narrow, rocky trail. How the hell did he know this trail was here? Jake wondered. The descent seemed interminable and impossible, but finally Nantan Lupan stepped into a cave alongside the rocky route. "We wait here until sun high in sky."

"Why wait?" Jake asked.

"Men grow sleepy in afternoon. Less attention. Then we attack."

Jake paused before speaking. He'd planned to ride up the canyon and commence with the shootout, maybe take out a lookout or two on the way in if he saw anyone. It wasn't much of a plan, but given the lay of the land, and short of sneaking into camp in the dark, he didn't have much choice. "We could start picking them off from up here," Jake said.

"Yes. But wait for sleep time of day. Gun belts come off. Rifles rest. Men slow. Maybe shoot each other." Nantan Lupan smiled. "Make job easier."

Come to think of it, he could use a bit of a nap himself, Jake realized.

Both heard hooves from far below and peeked cautiously over the edge of the narrow trail to find a changing of the guard underway.

Nantan Lupan strung an arrow. "Now good time to kill lookout. Arrow silent. One more gone."

With the precision of a surgeon's scalpel, Nantan Lupan's arrow found its mark, and the man dropped.

Jake waited patiently while the sun passed overhead. He always became patient and calm before a confrontation. Coldblooded is how someone had once described him. Since it might be his last day alive, he allowed himself to think of Betsy, and he found himself doing so in a more objective way than ever before.

He wondered if he was the right man for her. For some reason, he began to question that now. She wanted tradition – a home, baby, livestock, a man with her every night. Jake thrived on action. Raised on a cattle ranch, and later working as a drover, he found cattle tiresome. Horses required even more attention and ate up a man's life with training schedules, auctions, and equine ailments. Jake liked being in the saddle. He liked showdowns. He liked his Colt and his badge. They pleased him immensely; they did not please Betsy in the least.

Now, she carried his child, which complicated their situation. He could marry her, which would be the right thing to do, but she'd never be happy. Not really happy. And he'd never stand for being a house husband. He should probably go ahead and marry her and then let her divorce him later. Doing so would hurt her deeply, and he loved her despite their differences, but that plan might be for the best in the long run.

Betsy was beautiful, endearing, and irresistible. But that wasn't enough to change him – to change who he really was and what he really wanted out of life.

He'd known this all along, deep down. Maybe that's why he'd stalled at getting married. And stalled at staying with her when she'd begged him to. Hell, even McGraw had downright begged him not to leave her.

CANYON OF DEATH

He watched Nantan Lupan as the Indian sharpened arrowheads. "You miss Sophy?"

Nantan Lupan looked up, anger flashing in his eyes. "Speak not of Sophee. I may kill you yet, my friend."

"What are you going to do after this?" Jake asked.

"I go to Sonora with my woman. I stay. Never return to these mountains."

"Maybe I'll travel down that way someday," Jake said, thinking it might be sooner than later. "Where will I find you?"

"I will know when you come. I will find *you*," Nantan Lupan answered.

"When do you recommend we go in?" Jake asked, nodding toward the canyon.

"Canyon of death awaits. You will know when it is time."

The cryptic answers Nantan Lupan often gave irked Jake at times. A simple, straightforward reply would be helpful. "I'm going in this afternoon," Jake said unexpectedly. "The sun will be in my favor."

The Indian nodded in agreement.

"I want you to stay here," Jake said. "This is my fight. And the day comes that I can't kill five men by myself is a sad day indeed."

"Maybe more men than we see," Nantan Lupan responded.

"No matter. I go in alone."

Neither spoke for the next hour. Finally, Jake pushed to his feet. "I'm going to cross to the other side of the canyon and swipe the lookout's horse. Can't walk into this thing. Take all damn day."

"Now you think like me." Nantan Lupan smiled. "Smart man."

Jake retraced his steps a few hundred yards up the narrow trail they'd recently descended and cut across the hillside to the other side of the canyon. None below seemed the wiser. No one suspected an approach from over the top of the mountain, and the afternoon tiredness was stealing upon them as Nantan Lupan had predicted.

Quietly scrambling from one scrawny bush to another, taking every precaution not to be seen by the dozing men in the canyon, Jake heard the approach of a horse from below and stopped a hundred yards from the dead lookout. Sure enough, a replacement lookout had come. Before the man could spin the horse about and gallop off to tell the others of their dead comrade, however, another of Nantan Lupan's arrows struck its victim, and the rider toppled silently to the ground.

    Jake slipped toward the two prone men. Removing a dead man's hat and marveling at the lethal arrows sticking out of the men's craws, Jake mounted one of the horses and began working his way down the hillside. He hoped that by wearing one of the men's hats, and with the sun in their eyes, he'd look familiar enough that the men in camp wouldn't be the wiser until he was much too close for them to react. Jake looked up the hillside and saw Nantan Lupan watching. Slouching in the saddle, he rode on.

DOWN

Jake eased down the incline to the bottom of the canyon. Head held steady, his eyes swept side to side, searching for any other posted lookouts he may not have seen from above. He carried his rifle in his right hand, held firmly against his leg. Thanks to Nantan Lupan, three outlaws had been taken down – the Indian who'd forced the girl into the bushes, and the two with arrows through their gullets. He wondered how many men Johnny had brought along. Even now, from a distance, he could clearly see three horses. He knew that Johnny had been accompanied by two Navajos and two outlaws. That made five. Three lie dead, so there should only have been two horses, yet he saw three hobbled animals grazing not far from a smoldering campfire. "Three's not bad," he muttered. "I've bested three before. Hell, I've done four." But even as he tried to embolden himself, he knew that fast-draw Johnny Geiger had never been among the groups of men he'd killed.

The men, lazing about, paid no attention as Jake angled toward the hobbled horses and dismounted. It would be easier shooting if he didn't have to fire from the back of a horse. He had no way of knowing if the animal'd ever been fired from. Probably had, but if it hadn't, the result could be quite a circus.

Jake bent down as though hobbling the animal, then rose on the opposite side of the horse. Placing the horse between him and the outlaws, he propped the rifle on the saddle and drew a bead on one of the men. Should he give them a warning to throw down their weapons, or shoot them as they lie dozing, unarmed? He hesitated. He wanted to kill Geiger, but he wanted to do it in such a way that Johnny *knew – knew* who'd pulled the trigger. He wanted to look Geiger in the eye when he did it. Shooting like this would not give him the satisfaction of avenging Betsy.

"Everybody stand up. Put your hands up. You're under arrest!" he shouted. Why was he warning them? These were vermin. These men killed and robbed for a living.

"Why, if it isn't U.S. Deputy Marshal Jake Silver," drawled Geiger. "Good job, Marshal. You snuck in right smart. You done good. I'm impressed."

"You're under arrest, John Geiger, for attempted murder, kidnapping, and assault," Jake shouted. "Tell your friends to mount up and get out. I got no beef with them."

One of the men slowly moved his hand toward his gunbelt, but the movement did not escape Jake. He fired a warning shot, and the bullet blew off the end of the man's middle finger which sent him into a howling fit. "Move again, and I'll take your whole hand next time," Jake warned, walking slowly toward the three outlaws.

"My my. Ain't you somethin' special," Geiger taunted. "Shootin' unarmed men. Gotta say, I'm disappointed in you, Marshal."

"Shut up, Geiger. Keep your hands up. You two," Jake said, nodding toward the two accomplices but never taking his eyes off Geiger, "you guys get the hell out of here or make your peace. I only want Geiger. If you don't leave now, I can guarantee neither of you will leave this canyon alive."

A smile spread slowly over Geiger's face. "I believe you are mistaking, Marshal. It's you who won't be leaving alive."

Geiger's tone troubled Jake. Something was up. It was not until the bullet hit him in the back that he heard the report of the rifle. The shock of being hit caused him to momentarily go blank, long enough for the three scoundrels to grab their gunbelts and start firing. Jake stumbled to his knees and fell prostrate, still conscious but too stunned to respond.

Who the hell had been behind him? Jake wondered. With tremendous effort, he rolled onto his back. An Indian strode toward him. Not Nantan Lupan. A Navajo. Yes, the thought flitted through Jake's mind that there'd been two Navajos riding with Johnny. Nantan Lupan had only killed one.

Bullets peppered the ground, kicking sand, grit, and rock shards over him. The Navajo kept coming, rifle raised, preparing to fire another round into Jake's prostrate body, unaware that Jake remained conscious. With his left hand, Jake raised his rifle several inches and fired into the oncoming assailant's groin. The man stopped, disbelief sweeping over his face, sank to his knees, and grabbed at his groin as though holding it in place. That's when Jake's second bullet hit him in the chest.

Jake could hear Geiger in the background screaming for the two shooters to stop. "Stop, damn you! He's mine! I want to kill him!"

The shooting ceased, and Jake heard labored footsteps trudging through the sand coming toward him. The horses, alarmed at the barrage of bullets, hopped about wildly and screamed in fear. One crashed to the earth in front of Jake, affording him the opportunity to roll onto his stomach and retrieve the Colt from his gunbelt. It had taken every ounce of energy to do so, and sweat caused by pain and shock drenched him. He could feel the blood pulsing out of the hole in his back, but he felt no dampness on his shirt front. The bullet had not gone through, but lie lodged in his chest. At that moment he had no doubt he would die in this far-off canyon, but he was determined he'd not die until Geiger lay dead first.

Summoning every bit of strength, he waited. Johnny strode forth, brandishing his weapon and double checking the gun's loaded magazine. Though he had a clear shot, Jake waited, determined to see the man's eyes when he shot him.

Geiger looked up, a grin plastered on his face. Cocksure of his enemy's demise, he looked back at his friends and gave a shout of happiness. "Just like a turkey shoot, ain't it, boys?" he yelled. "I told you this sumbitch wasn't worth being scared of, didn't I? *Didn't I?* Now you can all tell the tale of how Johnny Geiger gunned down the great Marshal Jake Silver."

Despite his predicament, Jake had to laugh at Johnny's posturing. The effort to laugh, however, caused him excruciating pain, and he closed his eyes for a moment. When he opened them, Geiger stood, not ten feet away, his gun aimed at Jake's head.

"You didn't put murder in those charges you just arrested me for, law dawg," Geiger drawled. "That means your woman must've lived. Guess I'll have to pay her another visit."

Jake lifted his head and smiled. "Over my dead body."

Geiger laughed maniacally. "Silver, you got a sense of humor. Never seen it before." Then Geiger did as Jake figured he would. Geiger turned again and yelled at his cohorts, "Hey, he says it'll be over his dead body," and he laughed uproariously.

When he'd retrieved his Colt, Jake had buried his hand under a thin layer of sand and dirt. Held firmly in his grip, the tip of the Colt broke the surface just as Johnny turned around. Jake prayed the gun would not jam.

When Johnny turned back toward the Jake, his eyes widened in surprise. Without taking aim, he raised his weapon and quickly fired off two shots. Both flew wild. One passed over Jake's head and the other buried itself in the earth, a foot from Jake's face.

Simultaneously, Jake fired, and the ensuing blast assured him the gun had remained in working order. The bullet struck Geiger squarely between the eyes. Like a felled tree, Geiger slowly keeled over backward, his head bouncing off a rock, his arms flung wide.

It took a few seconds for the two desperadoes to understand that Geiger had just been shot. Aiming at one of the men, Jake pulled the trigger again, but the gun failed to fire a second time. Struggling with every last ounce of strength, he tried to retrieve the other Colt, but he found himself unable to move his arm enough to even pull the gun from its holster.

Wayward bullets again peppered him with rocks, dirt, and sand, neither desperado willing to approach closer after what had just happened to Geiger. A slug deflected off a large rock and tore into Jake's leg. He heard the bone crack, and he yelled out in pain.

Another shot hit his outstretched forearm, passing through, while a third grazed his head above his ear.

Suddenly the shooting stopped, and all Jake heard was the pounding of his heart and the sound of screaming, and then running feet. "Let it be over," he prayed. "Just let it be over."

***

Nantan Lupan watched Jake retrieve the horse and hat and ride to the canyon floor. Lying on his stomach and peering over the ledge, he saw Jake dismount and, while not able to hear words clearly, he heard Jake shout and a man respond. The Indian shook his head. Jake had them dead to rights; why would he tamper with good fortune by giving them a chance?

Suddenly, a shot rang out, but Nantan Lupan was not able to identify the shooter. He saw Jake go down, and then a moment later he saw an Indian come out from under a ledge.

Without hesitation, Nantan Lupan leaped from the narrow animal trail over the ledge of the precipice. Landing on the hard slope, he catapulted head first down the hill. He hit on his shoulder and then began sliding, rolling, tumbling down the hillside. Chunks of flesh peeled from his exposed skin. Even the deerskin clothing he wore could not protect him from rocks, stumps, and brush. He dared not spread his hands or grab at brush or cactus to arrest his fall lest he lose his weapons. His cheek smashed into a large rock, dazing him but slowing his descent enough for him to direct himself into a bush where his fall slowed even more.

Finally, coming to a stop, he groaned but did not stop moving. Leaping upright, he scrambled down the hillside, slipping and sliding, but angling toward the campsite.

Two more shots rang out, and Nantan Lupan saw the Indian fall. Good. Jake still lived. Nantan Lupan turned his attention to the three remaining men. Stumbling now, he reached the bottom of the steep slope. A swollen ankle slowed him, and he cursed. Still a distance from the campsite, he heard a solitary shot, then seconds later more gunfire erupted. Hobbling, he kept moving. The firing ceased, and he saw a lone gunman swagger toward Jake, pistol drawn. Nantan Lupan, well within rifle range, stopped to load and shoot, only to realize that the Sharps rifle he so prized had been somehow torn from his grip on his death-defying slide down the hillside. Relief coursed through him, however, when he felt his knife still in its leather case.

He must hurry, but he couldn't risk being seen. Grimacing, he began moving again, knowing now that he must absolutely kill the remaining men in retribution for murdering Jake Silver. Not believing his eyes, however, he saw the forward lone gunman collapse at almost the exact moment he heard the blast of Jake's Colt. Excitement coursing through him, he quickened his pace, the ankle now beyond pain. His friend yet lived.

CANYON OF DEATH

The cacophony of exploding rounds was deafening, so much so that the gunmen failed to hear Nantan Lupan's approach. Only when a knife stuck in one gunman's back causing him to collapse did the other gunman notice the wiry Apache pulling someone's shotgun from one of the saddles lying on the ground.

"No. I got no beef with you – or him either," Boots said, nodding toward Jake and backing away from Nantan Lupan despite the fact that he still held a loaded weapon.

Nantan Lupan could tell by the shotgun's weight that the weapon held no shells, but he advanced slowly toward the quaking shooter, pumping the gun as though a shell were in the chamber.

"No way did I shoot anyone. I missed on purpose. I never shot no one. I didn't want to be here anyway. I just pretended to be shooting. You gotta believe me," Boots said, quivering.

The outlaw continued easing away from the approaching Indian. Nantan Lupan grinned as he quickly took the shotgun by the barrel and swung the stock with all his strength, cold-cocking the man up the side of his head. Boots stumbled and keeled over backward into the smoldering campfire. Screaming, Boots struggled to roll off the fire, but Nantan Lupan stood atop him holding him face down. The flames leaped higher and Boots' skin sizzled and popped as his clothes smoked and burst into flame. His shrieks pierced the silence in the canyon. Nantan Lupan only stepped from the burning man's body when flames began to lick his own leg.

Hobbling to the fallen marshal, the Apache knelt. He counted at least three bullet wounds. Perhaps there were more. Surprised, he could see the marshal still breathed. Sitting cross legged beside his friend, the Indian rocked slowly back and forth, chanting for strong medicine and guidance.

TRAIL OF BLOOD

It took only a minute for Nantan Lupan to collect himself. He began ripping and tearing shirts and neck kerchiefs from the dead men's bodies. He must stem Jake's blood loss as best as he could. After binding Jake's wounds with the dirty garments, he bound his own swollen ankle and then set about retrieving the horses that had finally begun to settle down. He needed to get Jake out of the canyon. He couldn't care for him here. The thought that he might not be able to care for him at all weighed upon him, but he proceeded as though Jake would survive. If the man could live until Nantan Lupan got him to his camp, he stood a chance.

Getting Jake onto the horse took Nantan Lupan far longer than he expected and caused Jake such pain that he revived briefly, only to pass out once again. Pulling the much bigger man into the saddle took every ounce of the small, wiry Indian's strength. Blood seeped through the filthy bindings, but Nantan Lupan could not worry about the blood. He must keep Jake in the saddle at all cost. It would be a full day's ride back to the camp. Once there he could administer to Jake as best as he could. It would be another full day to the settler's house he'd passed many days before. If Jake survived the first leg of this journey, Nantan Lupan figured he could keep him alive to survive the second trip to the homestead.

Glancing at the sky, the Apache grew disheartened. Snow would fall soon. He noted the wind backing to the east. It would grow cold soon enough.

Ever practical, Nantan Lupan secured the remaining horses and quickly gathered the men's weaponry and supplies. It seemed a good sign that his friend opened his eyes periodically, once even nodding his head in what

CANYON OF DEATH

Nantan Lupan believed to be a sign of approval. The Indian spoke to him continually as the two men and the small remuda moved out of the canyon of death.

Someone would find the bodies. Stories would grow. Apaches would be blamed. Soldiers would come again.

It took many hours for them to return to camp, but had Nantan Lupan not known the area so thoroughly – every shortcut and animal trail – it would have taken more time yet. Nantan Lupan's woman rushed to his aid when he entered the small clearing. He'd left the string of horses outside the entry. Together they slowly lowered Jake to the ground and carried him to the protection of the ledge.

The fever had fallen upon him, and Jake shook with cold even as he burned with fire. Nantan Lupan, himself never ill, nonetheless knew the power of leaves and stems from various plants. He carried a small amount of these in a pouch, and when his woman saw what he needed, she nodded and left the shelter to search for more. The ocotillo would provide a good poultice, but it did not flourish this far south. Still, other plants could be harvested that might prove helpful.

Through the night both Indians kept watch over Jake. After cleaning his wounds, Nantan Lupan applied a dark, stinking salve to them, hoping to draw poisons out. The wound on Jake's head, although an angry red, already looked to be scabbing over, and the arm the bullet had pierced did not appear to be festering. But the wounds to his leg and back looked fearful and troublesome. Only the fact that Jake did not gurgle when he breathed or seep blood from his mouth gave the Apache hope that all was not lost.

The two alternated caring for him, one always at his side. Nantan Lupan left camp only to retrieve the two horses he and Jake had left at the base of the mountain. He returned with cold spring water and a small deer for them to eat and for the woman to make a broth of the innards for Jake.

The temperature plummeted as the first snow came to the Chiricahuas earlier than usual. Wrapping Jake in all the available blankets, he still shook with cold while burning hot. Applying cool compresses to his face and neck helped the rampaging fever quell, but both saw the big man's decline within two days of his being under their care.

"I must go to the white man's house," Nantan Lupan abruptly announced early on the morning of the third day. He paused, knowing that the woman spoke another tongue and could not understand him. To his surprise, however, she responded, speaking a mixture of Navajo and Apache. He understood her completely despite the blending of the two tongues, not all that dissimilar.

"You must take the white man with you," she said. "He will not live long enough for you to go and return."

Nantan Lupan nodded. The woman spoke truth. With snow on the ground, it could be a day's ride to the homestead. A day's journey back, and the possibility he would not be able to raise the help Jake needed. But if he took Jake along, no one would refuse to assist. She had spoken wisely, and Nantan Lupan felt a surge of gladness that his woman could understand such things. He looked at her with new regard, and she came to his side, placing her hand upon his chest.

"Quickly. Or your friend may die tomorrow."

Nantan Lupan nodded again. Without a word being spoken, she began helping him prepare for the journey. Somehow, Jake must be gotten into the saddle and kept upright. In his failing condition, however, he would not be able to sit alone. She would have to assist in Jake's transport.

Carefully, they stowed the extra blankets and other goods Jake had given them. Although trespassers were unlikely given the time of year and the secrecy of the campsite, Nantan Lupan did not want to lose these valuable commodities. They briefly contemplated how to wrestle Jake into the saddle, and quickly realized the impossibility of doing so given his size, failing condition, and inability to help in the least. In exasperation and fear of injuring him further, they quickly assembled a travois on which to lay him. The travois wouldn't give him the smoothest ride, but it would be better than trying to keep him upright in the saddle. His leg wound started to bleed copiously again, and now Nantan Lupan could see a jagged bone poking out the side of the limb.

At the last minute Nantan Lupan penned the extra horses he'd taken inside the small enclosure, but he attached the travois to the unruly mule. He would not have such a creature remain in his camp.

CANYON OF DEATH

***

When not hallucinating, Jake awoke for brief periods and watched the two Indians hovering about, tending him. Surprised he still lived, he didn't harbor any hope that he'd hold out much longer. Although the pain in his back had subsided to a dull throb, his leg seared in merciless agony. Moving it caused excruciating pain when the tip of the broken bone poked into his muscle and flesh. If only he could keep the leg immobile. Without being told, he knew it to be broken. *So this is what a broken leg feels like,* flitted through his mind before he again drifted off.

He awoke sometime later, time now being meaningless to a dying man, and watched soft, white snowflakes spiraling down. He smiled, marveling at the sight, and wondered momentarily if he might be in heaven until the travois jolted, causing an intense spasm of pain. No, if he could still feel the pain, he hadn't died yet, he assured himself. But the beauty of the falling snow soon arrested his attention again when the pain had passed. His mind roamed, and he did not know he wandered in and out of consciousness, only that he'd never seen anything as beautiful as what he now saw. *Perhaps I should ride along the ground all the time,* he mused.

Never had the air smelled more pure and cold and clean. Tears rolled down his cheeks at the sheer beauty of everything within sight. *I'm dying,* he thought. *Dying is not so bad. Far more pleasant that it's given credit for.* He could not drink in enough of the splendor around him. Never had snow seemed so dazzling, so lovely. So magnificent. A flake fell into his eye and he smiled with childlike happiness. Its delicious coldness made him blink. Breathing deeply, he tried to treasure the delectable air, but the breath caused him to cough – which caused his back to hurt so bad he could hardly bear the pain.

Where am I going? he wondered. *Am I on the road to heaven?* Jake had never been a believer, but now he wondered if there remained sufficient time to rethink his agnostic ways. The sheer beauty of the world he saw convinced him he did not travel the road to hell. He closed his eyes, feeling icy coldness on his cheeks, and snowflakes occasionally kissing his face. A mule brayed, and he suddenly understood he was being transported by someone to somewhere. But who, where, and why escaped him. *Wild Bill's alive at least,* he thought. *How did I get here? What happened to me?*

Slowly, he began to recall the gunfight in the canyon. He saw the Indian fall. And Johnny Geiger. *But what had happened to the rest?* And then he knew for a certainty that Nantan Lupan must have appeared. Again the Apache he'd not deemed worthy enough for his sister, Sophy, had saved his life.

His eyes closed.

***

The journey to the white man's cabin took all day, and Nantan Lupan kept a close eye on Jake. At times Jake seemed lucid, and once Nantan Lupan saw him smiling and looking about appreciatively. These motions perplexed him, although he had seen many elders do such odd things as their time to pass approached.

It was a day for much introspection. The soft, downy flakes and crystal cold air invigorated even the most flagging of spirits and brought forth long-forgotten memories. Despite the urgency of Jake's situation, Nantan Lupan found himself gazing about in appreciation for everything he saw. He remained wary for any other travelers who might appear, but because of the weather, none did.

He remembered other big snowfalls in the Chiricahuas. While beautiful, the snow brought much misery to his people who had to compete for what little game remained in the area. Often he would steal beef to help the members of his tribe subsist. Even though the Indians did not like the taste of the white man's cattle, it filled their bellies. Now, of course, he had only himself and his woman to feed. He looked over to the woman who rode the mule that pulled the travois, and felt a stirring in his heart. She was young, lithe, and pleasing to look upon. She'd had many chances to leave his camp, but she'd stayed. He hoped she'd stay forever. She clung to him at night, and welcomed his embrace and lovemaking. He could not ask for more.

What would her name be? he wondered. He thought he might call her Snowflake, since the white flakes looked beautiful against her black hair. But surely she had a tribal name.

"Woman, by what name are you called?" he asked, studying her.

"My name is Tiponi, Child of Importance. I was so named by my grandmother. My grandfather is our tribe's medicine man. My mother died in childbirth. I was to be a boy child."

CANYON OF DEATH

"You are better as a girl." Nantan Lupan smiled, surprising himself with the attention he gave her. "Tiponi. Good name. I call you Tiponi. I am Nantan Lupan. Greywolf."

"I know," she said. "I've heard you so called. Your name is known among my people. You are the last of the free Apaches."

To be known by others seemed a good thing, Nantan Lupan thought. He sat straighter and looked sterner, as though he would be more deserving of the honor.

The two rode in silence for some time, both keeping a close eye on the failing marshal. Finally, Nantan Lupan spoke. "White man house ahead. Be watchful. This man good, but maybe soldiers in the area. Wait here. If all is safe, I will signal."

Tiponi slipped from the mule and knelt momentarily by the travois. "Hurry, Nantan Lupan. Not much time remains." Then she did as bid.

Nantan Lupan approached the house with caution. Smoke wafted from the stone chimney, and the snow held only one man's tracks to a woodpile and back to the dwelling. A small light shone through a window pane. Fearful of approaching too close, Nantan Lupan stopped before the house and waited. Almost immediately he heard the front door open a crack.

"What do you want?" a man's voice called out.

"Marshal need help. Many shots by outlaw," Nantan Lupan replied.

The door opened wider and the homesteader stepped onto the porch, a rifle in his arms. Sure enough, he spotted the travois carrying the body and called to his wife, "Emma, get some more hot water going. We got an injured man out here."

Setting the rifle inside the door, the man ran to the mule, Nantan Lupan following close behind. Looking up, the man said, "Help me get him inside. No one here will hurt you. You must be Jake's friend. He told us about you. You're safe here."

Nantan Lupan unhooked the travois from the mule. The two men pulled it through the snow, up the few steps to the porch, and through the cabin door. The ground over which they pulled the travois showed a trail of bright red blood.

GOODBYE

Much concern and confusion reigned when the two men carried the marshal in. It took all of them to get Jake lifted from the travois and laid on a cot. Although Neil Erickson and his wife were not medical practitioners, life on the frontier had prepared them for minor catastrophes. Major injuries had never occurred, so neither felt confident to remove the bullet embedded in Jake's back. Neil thought, however, that he could set and splint the leg. But if infection had already set in, that would be another matter. He'd seen men die from broken legs during his time in the military. *Something* had to be done, however, because it looked to be the most dodgy injury – worse, it seemed, than the bullet hole in Jake's back and arm. He didn't want to see the marshal lose a leg, and lose it he might if something weren't done right soon. Might be too late as it was.

Erickson questioned whether he should set the leg, but he couldn't see letting the marshal lie there in agony. Setting the bone wouldn't make it worse, of that he felt certain. Might help relieve the pain.

Carefully, he removed the dirty wrap the Indian had bound over the break. The noxious, putrid smell of the gaping wound made all of them pull back and turn their heads away. "Emma, bring me that pan of hot water and a clean rag," Neil said after he caught his breath. You got any laudanum?"

"Got a whole bottle from Doctor Silas when we were last in Maley," Emma answered, scurrying to a cupboard to retrieve the opium.
"Let's give him a good draught of that. It'll make the pain subside, and make what I'm gonna do a lot less painful. Not sure if this leg should be set or cut off, but I'll leave any cuttin' to a doctor. No harm in tryin' to save it while we can."

CANYON OF DEATH

***

Nantan Lupan stood by the door, watching the proceedings. He'd already signaled for Tiponi to join him, and the woman entered the house so silently neither of the Ericksons were aware of her presence.

Emma Erickson carefully spooned the laudanum into Jake's mouth, giving him far more than was prescribed.

"We'll wait just a few minutes for that to take effect," Erickson said aloud, "then we'll set this leg. Let's clean it up first. See what we got here."

Despite the horrible stench, once Erickson removed the black goo Nantan Lupan had applied, the wound did not look the least infected, leastwise not enough to call for amputation. "What in tarnation is this black stuff?" he asked, realizing the stench came from the medication the Indian had applied, not Jake's wound.

"Apache medicine," Nantan Lupan replied.

"This stuff stinks like hell, but it looks like it works right fine. I don't see any infection – leastwise not on the outside. Could be trouble that we just can't see though."

After a few minutes, Erickson deemed the time right to set the leg. "Marshal, you might feel this. Hope you don't, but we're gonna try and set this leg now anyway. You'll be in a lot less pain once it's done. Emma, and you – " he looked toward Nantan Lupan and noticed Tiponi for the first time. "You two hold him in case he tries to move. Hold him good, now. This could hurt like hell."

The three secured Jake, and Erickson, after studying the break, proceeded to set the leg. He gave a couple of violent tugs, leaving Jake groaning with teeth clenched.

"For god's sake, man. It's set," Jake finally roared. "I can't take anymore!"

"Yep. I think we're good, Marshal. You lie right still," Neil said, looking at his handiwork and seeing that the bone was no longer visible. "We're going to dress that wound and splint the leg so's you can't move it. You need more of that laudanum, you let Emma know."

"Give me the damn bottle," Jake growled.

Emma hesitated, and reluctantly handed the bottle to the marshal, who upended it, drinking the entire contents.

"Hope you don't die from drug overdose," Neil commented wryly.

"That's the least of my worries," Jake responded, slurring slightly.

After Jake fell into a deep sleep, Neil rebandaged the wound in Jake's arm. It, too, looked like it was on the road to mending, leastwise he could see no infected-looking areas. He then announced he'd be going to Fort Bowie to fetch a doctor. "We still got that bullet in the back to deal with. I'm amazed he ain't died from that one. I need to leave at first light."

He turned to address Nantan Lupan and the woman. "You're welcome to stay. I know the marshal is your friend. We ain't got much room in the cabin, but there's a nice, dry place in the barn if you want to bed down there. You're welcome to take your meals with us."

Nantan Lupan nodded. "We stay."

"Would you care for some tea?" Emma asked, an uncertain look on her face, not knowing the proper protocol for visiting Indians. "Have a seat. I'll make us some tea," she said, pulling out a chair and motioning for Tiponi to be seated. Though Tiponi spoke only a few words of English, the women sat and drank tea while Erickson showed Nantan Lupan the barn and where to put up the animals.

When the men were alone, Erickson asked the Indian what had transpired.

"Many men want kill marshal. Canyon of Death. One man shoot marshal in back. Others shoot at him. Marshal kill two. I kill more."

Erickson nodded. "I'm wondering if these are the men who rode through here a coupla weeks ago."

"Same men. No others travel in mountains this late."

"Listen, Nantan Lupan, if I bring the doctor from the fort, soldiers will probably accompany him. You might not be safe here."

"We wait in woods. If no soldiers, we stay. Soldiers come, they no see Nantan Lupan."

"Fair enough. Just wanted to warn ya, is all."

Jake remained unconscious through the evening. The laudanum also lowered his temperature, so he no longer hallucinated or thrashed about. Nantan Lupan and Tiponi retired to the barn, choosing not to eat with the whites. Instead, they ate jerky and drank water.

CANYON OF DEATH

Erickson left the following morning before dawn. It was a distance to the fort and back, but Nantan Lupan took no chances on being apprehended, so he and Tiponi returned to their camp early to gather their belongings and prepare for their journey south. Nantan Lupan had decided to leave for Mexico once he knew if Jake would recover – or if he would die.

It was not until the following evening that Erickson returned with the doctor. As Erickson had anticipated, a small military escort accompanied the two men. Nantan Lupan watched their arrival from a safe distance.

***

In the cabin, Jake had regained consciousness. He told Ericson and the doctor he might be marginally better, but pain still wracked him when he moved.

The doctor studied Jake's leg closely. "Nice job, Neil," he said. "I couldn't have done better myself at setting this thing. Nasty break. Unfortunately, the bullet remains inside the leg, as I see no exit wound at all. Of course, I suppose it could have ricocheted out. Still, if no infection has set in, we may be in the clear with this wound."

"How will you know if it's in there, doc?" Jake asked.

"Well, most bullets are inherently dirty from gun powder and being handled with filthy hands. Since the wound isn't infected, in may not be in there, although it probably is. When you're on your feet again, however, it's possible you may feel it. Bullets can stray, surprisingly enough. You may experience pain later near the surface of your leg, or if the shell pokes into a muscle or tendon. You might consider having it removed then."

"I'm certain the bullet hit me after bouncing off a rock," Jake said, wondering if that would make any difference.

The doctor did not respond, but simply continued to look the leg over and then moved on to the arm. He said nothing further about those injuries.

"What about your back, Jake? Neil tells me you were shot in the back," the doctor finally said.

"Yeah. Rifle. The bullet didn't come out, though. I'm sure it's lodged."

"That's not good, but it happens. We'll need to roll you over so we can examine the wound. Moving you will cause more pain, unfortunately."

Jake grimaced. He'd had about all the pain he could handle. "Got any more of that laudanum?" he asked.

"I'll give you some later if we operate," the doctor replied. "You best not use it now. I hear you already drank an entire bottle full. We don't want to turn you into an opium eater."

Neil and two of the soldiers carefully rolled Jake over, trying to keep his leg from twisting in any way. Jake erupted in a cold sweat from the pain.

The doctor peeled away Nantan Lupan's binding, and again a foul odor permeated the room. "The leg smelled that way, too, Doc, when I removed the wrapping, but it's okay," Neil said, looking on with interest. "The odor comes from that black salve, whatever it is."

"Open the door, will you? We need to get this stink out of here," the doctor responded, not impressed with the testimonial.

The bullet wound had begun closing, there being only a dark, red circle around the hole. After cleaning the wound, the doctor hesitated a few moments before speaking.

"Jake, the wound is closing on its own, but the bullet's lodged inside. I'd like to try and remove it."

"Why?"

"It, too, can move about in time. Eventually, it could puncture your lung, even gravitate to your heart. In either case, you'd die."

"But it *could* stay right where it is, couldn't it?" Jake asked, looking for a way to avoid more pain.

"Yes, but that's not too likely, given your lifestyle. There's also a small risk of lead poisoning, as the bullet can, and most likely will, rust in time."

"I heard of a guy with five bullets in him, and he didn't die from any of them," Jake responded.

"The decision is yours, Jake. I can try to dig the bullet out. There's no guarantee I can get to it, I'll be honest. Or we can let the wound mend as it's already tending to do."

"Leave well enough alone, Doc. I'll have something to remember this little episode by."

"Well, you may have a limp from that leg of yours to help you remember."

"How bad a limp?" Jake asked, truly concerned.

CANYON OF DEATH

"Every case is different. You're young. Strong. If you allow the leg to heal and then work it carefully, it may not give you any trouble at all. But I've seen some men with a stiff leg that troubles them the rest of their days."

The doctor proceeded to dress Jake's wound, then gave instructions to Emma and Neil on what to do and look for. "Bring him to the fort when he can travel. We'll take care of him there," the doctor said. "I'll leave you more laudanum. Let him use it for pain, but only sparingly."

Much to Jake's relief, the doctor and his escorts left the next morning. "Something about that man just makes me nervous," Jake commented as the men rode away. "I don't want to go to the fort, Neil. I can pay you for keeping me here. I know I'll be a nuisance, but I'd like to stay with the two of you, if you don't mind."

Neil nodded. "You are welcome here, Marshal. We shall enjoy the company, but also your friends can see you if you stay."

Jake hadn't noticed the absence of Nantan Lupan and his woman, but suddenly he realized that it had to have been they who'd brought him to the Erickson's. "Where are they?" he asked.

"I'm sure they'll be back once the doctor and his escorts are well away." Neil smiled. "That one moves like the shadows."

Toward evening Nantan Lupan and Tiponi returned. No one could misread the relief written on the Apache's face when he saw Jake awake and alert.

"Good. You live."

"Thanks to you," Jake said, gratitude in his eyes.

Nantan Lupan stood silently and nodded. Finally, he spoke. "My friend, it is time I journey south. I leave never to return."

"I understand."

"We have many...." Nantan Lupan stopped, searching for the words. "Many hard rides together. You. Me."

Jake reflected on the friendship that had developed against all odds between the two of them in the Arizona desert months ago when he'd journeyed there looking for his sister. There'd been the chase across the burning country after Nantan Lupan had taken Sophy. Then the shooting took place. Jake figured he'd never see the Indian again after they'd left him under a ledge with food and water to recover from his wounds.

Then Jake had run across the Apache camped near the cabin where Sophy'd spent so many months alone after John Wesley died in an Indian raid led by Nantan Lupan. Again, the Indian had showed up when Jake had been ambushed on the trail leading home to Prescott. And now, once again, the two had met in the Chiricahuas where Jake had gone to hunt his nemesis, Johnny Geiger. He clearly owed Nantan Lupan for his life.

"When will you leave?" Jake asked.

"With the new moon. Snow will stop for three days."

How the hell could he know that? Jake wondered. But then, how the hell had he come up with the stinking concoction that kept his wounds from festering and rotting?

"You staying here until then?"

Nantan Lupan looked toward Erickson, who nodded in assent.

"Stay. Prepare for journey with Tiponi. Woman named Tiponi. Child of Importance."

Tiponi? Jake had heard that name before. Yes, at the trading post. The old Indian woman by Betsy's side had called Betsy's baby Tiponi. Child of Importance. Jake looked with renewed interest at the girl standing behind Nantan Lupan.

Jake smiled, but did not feel the least happy. "Good. That sounds good." He closed his eyes, not wanting to see the Indian before him, his only friend. With Indians one never really knew where one stood with them. Especially Apaches. A deep sadness swept over him. *I'm just tired,* he thought. Thankfully, he heard Nantan Lupan leave. *Can't let that little bugger see me break down and cry.*

Jake slept for two days, and then for the first time since being shot he awoke hungry. "Think I'm gonna live, Emma," he announced as the woman brought him a cup of broth.

"An appetite is a sure sign," she smiled.

She helped him sit up, and even though he winced in discomfort, he had to admit he felt remarkably good, all things considered. "That laudanum does a man good," he commented. Being warm and safe probably had a lot to do with it also, he decided. And a crystal blue sky with a bright sun did much to revive his spirits.

He heard Wild Bill bray. Damn, he was growing to love that critter.

"I see Nantan Lupan brought the mule back," Jake commented.

"Yes, and your horse, too."

"Is Nantan Lupan still here?"

"Yes. He says they'll leave tomorrow."

"I'd like to see him before he leaves, if you don't mind."

"I'll have Neil tell him when he comes in," she said, pouring more broth into Jake's cup.

A moment later the door opened, and Neil Erickson pushed through with an armload of wood and a small pine tree. "That Indian's been cuttin' wood for two days. I won't have to cut any for the rest of the winter, I do believe."

"Neil, I'd like to see Nantan Lupan before he leaves. Could you tell him?"

"Sure. He don't talk much, do he?"

"Not much. But what he says is worth hearing," Jake answered.

Jake watched Emma hang handmade decorations on the tiny tree that afternoon. He'd forgotten about Christmas – and Thanksgiving, too, it seemed. He wondered if Betsy had given birth yet. He felt sure she had, though he wished otherwise. Would she be worried about him, or too angry to care? He would send her a letter. Neil could mail it from the fort or from Maley when he next went to town. What could he possibly tell her, though? He'd promised her he'd be there for the baby's birth, and he wasn't.

Nantan Lupan entered the house, breaking Jake's morose train of thought. "I heard you're leaving tomorrow," Jake said, sitting up.

"New moon."

"So you say." Jake paused, not sure how to say what he wanted, and decided on a direct approach. "Nantan Lupan, I want you to take my horse. It's yours. It's my gift to you."

"Black horse?"

"Yes. It's yours. Apache is yours."

Nantan Lupan smiled broadly. "I call him Jake. New name."

Jake grinned in return. "A most excellent name for a good horse."

"You keep mule," Nantan Lupan said, grinning slyly. "My gift."

"I think you already gave me a gift – the gift of life," Jake answered.

"I see you no more, brother. Let our memories always ride with us," Nantan Lupan said, turning serious.

"Goodbye, Nantan Lupan. Take care of yourself."

The Indian nodded to him, then to Emma who watched the scene, teary-eyed.

Morning found tracks leaving from the barn, and Wild Bill braying for his equine companion, Apache.

NANTAN LUPAN

Nantan Lupan and Tiponi stopped only briefly at their campsite to gather the hidden stores they'd stashed earlier. He looked over his treasures with pride. He now had good medicine. Plenty good medicine. Had he a tribe to return to, he would be heralded as a chief upon his homecoming when the tribesmen counted his weapons, blankets, and horses. Since he had no tribe anymore, however, he consoled himself that he would have good protection now, and could use the items for trade once in Mexico.

Picking out the best horse among those taken from the outlaws, Nantan Lupan saddled it for Tiponi. He himself never used the white man's sitting device, but he could readily see that it might prove useful. He fashioned a halter for Tiponi, and tied some of the blanket rolls behind the saddle. He spread the weapons and other goods among the remaining horses, that way if one got away he wouldn't lose everything by placing it all on one animal.

It grew late as Nantan Lupan and Tiponi packed the goods. Averse to traveling at night, he reluctantly told Tiponi they would stay one more night in the camp and leave before dawn. That meant he had only two days before the storm came, but if they pushed, the two could still make it out of the path of the storm and escape the worst of the its fury. If not, they could wait it out. He would find shelter.

He slept little that night, thinking of his future life in Mexico. Since he would no longer return to this land he loved, he would make his dwelling in Mexico more permanent. Perhaps he could build an adobe structure. Tiponi could plant a garden. Yet, wanderlust lay heavy on him. He'd once said he would ride until there was no more land. He had no idea how far that would be. But he'd been alone then. Now he had Tiponi. He must think on this.

CANYON OF DEATH

If he built an adobe, his life would be a different. But could he live among the Mexicans? He could speak some Spanish, but he didn't know if Tiponi could. Mexicans did not like Apaches.

Confused as to his future course of action, he lay back and watched the winter sky speckled with blinking stars. Why had this upheaval come to pass? The white man. The white man had come, bringing his evil ways, his sickness, his greed. The white people destroyed the land. They cut trees to build wood houses, houses that could not be moved without great trouble. Their cattle overgrazed the grasslands. Some tended sheep that ate the grass to the very dirt. These men killed wildlife, often for sport, leaving the rotting carcasses for coyotes and wolves, and then they killed even them. They had already killed off the buffalo. Nantan Lupan had never seen a buffalo, but he had heard of the great herds that once thundered across the world. White men's weapons were not honorable and showed no courage in a man, unlike the Indian, who squarely faced his foe and fought as men should.

The white man, whose greed was as big as the sky, would destroy the earth, just like the vile locusts that had once invaded the land and left not a twig.

Agitated, Nantan Lupan awoke Tiponi. "It is time," he said. Although still dark, the sun would awaken during the time it would take to pack up and get mounted.

They moved out slowly, watching for icy patches. The cold night air refreshed him, and he vowed to leave the misery brought on by the white man behind him. If needed, he would ride nonstop until he found a place where he and Tiponi could live safely, without harassment or threat.

As they approached the canyon of death that afternoon, Nantan Lupan slowed. Perhaps he should look, one more time, to see if there yet remained any valuables among the dead. The freezing weather would have preserved their bodies, so rotting carrion would not disgust him. But he knew it to be an evil canyon, and he hesitated. He and Tiponi did not have the leisure to dally, for the storm would come after another day. It would be a bad one, but it would be the last of the winter season. Perhaps they should make camp in the canyon, in a protected spot, and wait it out. He'd have time then to rummage through the dead men's belongings. Often, he knew from experience, they hid money in their boots. He could take scalps, which would add to his medicine. He would be very strong.

Still, he hesitated. Some foreboding swept over him, and he sat for a moment, struggling with his indecision.

He turned to leave, but almost immediately turned back again. "We go to canyon of death," he said to Tiponi. "My medicine bigger than canyon of death."

He saw a worried look on the girl's face. "Your medicine the greatest of all, Nantan Lupan, but I beg you, please do not go. In my dream I see bad men. They will kill you and take me."

Nantan Lupan pulled the spyglass he'd taken from one of the men from the pack. Even though inexpert at using it, he tried to act as though he used the item every day.

***

"Chancey! Indians! I seen two of 'em ridin' off way out there," said the lookout, a new recruit to the gang of outlaws.

"All of two, huh?" Chancey replied.

"Should I chase 'em down and shoot 'em?"

"Now why would you want to go and do something like that? The blast alone could cause an avalanche in this canyon." Chancey retrieved his own stolen spyglass from a saddlebag and peered down the length of the canyon. Two Indians had stopped at the mouth of the canyon. It looked to be a man and a woman with a string of horses. Chancey, despite his vile nature, categorically did not believe in shooting women, regardless of origin. Unlike his fellow bandits, Chancey had one decent trait. Hurting women was off limits, and he would not tolerate it among his crew. Although friendly with Johnny Geiger, Chancey had strongly objected to Geiger's treatment of gals. Chancey couldn't abide it, and he'd almost shot Geiger in the back once because of it. But, someone else had taken the cussed gunman out, and Chancey felt no remorse.

"I don't think they're aware of us…yet. No Indian in his right mind would approach with us here. I wonder what they want. Maybe they're diseased or something," Chancey said. "Stand ready, but no one fires till I give the signal. Hide behind the rocks. Again, NO ONE FIRES or you'll answer to me."

The men did as bid, and Chancey watched the two sit for a minute as though in conversation.

***

In the cold, snowy canyon the leader's voice, though low, reached Nantan Lupan. Surprised that men would be here, he looked about and belatedly saw where a lookout had been posted. Tracks in the snow indicated so. Finally, he held the glass correctly and made out a handful of horses hidden at the head of the canyon. Angry with himself for his lack of attention while thinking of more treasure, he stopped, calculating whether to withdraw or to continue on and kill the white men. If he fled, he figured he and Tiponi might be pursued. If he went forward, it would mean a different kind of death. If the men were military, he'd be taken to the reservation and all of his goods confiscated. If they were outlaws, he'd be outnumbered and would probably be scalped and burned alive in retribution for the dead. Tiponi would be violated by the men and left to freeze. Although he knew his good medicine might assure him of victory, he did not want to lose the biggest amount of loot he'd ever had

He spoke in a low voice. "Tiponi, we are watched. Men here. We are out of their range for now, unless a man have a keen eye and steady hand. Once I signal, ride with the wind. We must escape this canyon."

The girl nodded, terrified of capture. All Indians knew what white men did to Indian women.

A day later Nantan Lupan and Tiponi passed into Mexico. Although Texas Rangers and the military regularly violated the sanctity of the international border, Nantan Lupan silently breathed a sigh of relief. He would head to his mountain cave for the remainder of the winter and decide which path he would take – the path to the end of land, or the path to a settled life among the Mexicans. If he settled, he would have to find a village where he and his woman could live in peace. He again vowed never to see his native land. He looked at the girl who rode beside him, but slightly behind as custom dictated. With her, he had no need to return.

A young girl, perhaps half his age, she might soon be with child, and Nantan Lupan wanted boy children he could teach the ways of the Apache to. Many boy children, but perhaps a girl, too. He looked at Tiponi and nodded his approval. His young, beautiful woman brought him great honor.

He thought of his friend, Jake, and the half-wild, black stud he now rode that Jake had given him. A man with a horse such as this had great medicine. Once the two mares in his small remuda came into season, the stud would mate with them. He could have a fine string of horses in time and become a trader. Maybe the adobe house would not be so bad, he thought. Especially with Tiponi by his side. He had waited long to have a wife and children. Tiponi prepared his meals and his bed. She warmly greeted him in the night when he came to her. And she was a clever girl, surprising him by speaking Spanish more fluently than even he spoke, having learned it from the priests who'd converted the Indians on the reservations. She was blessed with a second sight, also.

Approaching a ridge, a light snow falling, Nantan Lupan reined his great horse to a stop. He sat, looking over the terrain, and a smile such as he'd not worn since a child, spread slowly across his face.

A CHANGE OF HEART

For two weeks Betsy lay in bed recovering from the difficult birth. The puny infant, born prematurely from what Doc Watkins could determine, wasn't expected to live. Under Virginia and Sophy's constant care, however, the baby girl had somehow survived and begun to thrive. Too morose to take an active interest in her daughter, Betsy simply fed the baby when needed, but left the child's care to others.

After two weeks of putting up with Betsy's sulking and prolonged recuperation, Virginia Hall thought it time to have a talk. "Betsy, it's a lovely day. Let's open these windows and let some fresh air in for a bit. It's cold out, but some nice, clean air will do you a world of good," she said, fighting with the stubborn window, now half frozen closed. She turned to see tears trickling down Betsy's cheeks. "What is it, dear?"

When no answer came, Virginia again spoke. "Betsy, we need to talk. You must talk about what ails you. It's the only way you'll feel any better. Doctor Watkins says you're in perfect health – all things considered," she added quickly. "Come, now. What's upsetting you so?" Virginia had no doubt what ailed Betsy, but she feared to bring up the subject herself. She thought it best if Betsy brought up the unmentionable.

"He wasn't here," Betsy finally said. "He said he'd be here. He promised me. I'll never forgive him for this!"

"Betsy, no one knew you were so far advanced in your time," Virginia said, trying to soothe the girl. "It didn't look as if the baby was at all ready to be born. I'm sure if Jake would have known you were only a few weeks from delivery, he would have made a different decision."

"It wouldn't have mattered, Virginia. Nothing matters to him but being a marshal and running all over the countryside," Betsy retorted.

"Nonsense, Betsy. Utter nonsense. Anyone can tell that Jake cares for you deeply."

"If he cares for me so deeply, then why didn't he marry me when he could have? I'm humiliated, Virginia. Everyone who looks at me knows I am without a husband. I'm mortified and can't bear to show my face outside this house!"

"Dear, I don't want to lecture you, but these are things you should have thought about before…before you engaged in conjugal relations. That is why marriage is so important…." Virginia trailed off, sorry that she'd begun to preach to the girl.

"Besides, it's nonsense, Betsy. Very few people know you were with child. You are not the center of gossip in Prescott, I assure you."

In point of fact, polite society in Prescott had been quite interested in Betsy's personal affairs, given her unprecedented arrival in town over a year ago with the eligible young marshal. Dressed as a boy, she'd garnered a great deal of attention at the time, and she'd continued to do so, what with her vast inheritance from Shaun Agar, her hiring a black overseer and ranch hand to live on her property when she alone lived on the ranch, and her titilating dalliance with Jake Silver. The delivery of a child was almost to be expected, considering her ignorance of proper social conduct.

"Listen to me, Betsy. I speak only out of love. What I am going to say may be painful, but I say it with only your best interests in mind." Virginia paused, fearing what she planned to say might cause a rift between her and the girl. "May I speak to you openly and not fear your enmity?"

Betsy nodded. "I just don't want you to think I'm a bad person, Virginia. You've been like a mother to me. I don't want to risk losing your friendship."

"I will never desert you, Betsy. But what I'm going to tell you may not be pleasant for you to hear." Virginia cleared her throat and sat down on the edge of the bed. "Betsy, what has happened to you is not the end of the world. You are not the only girl who has found herself in this predicament, and you must prepare yourself for the fact that Jake may not marry you as he says he will. I know he says he intends to do so, but you need to ask yourself if he is the right man for you."

Betsy's eyes grew large at Virginia's suggestion. She started to shake her head and protest, but Virginia did not let her interrupt. "I do not doubt for one minute that Jake loves you madly, and that you love him. But I, for one, do not think you are well matched, dear. He is a lawman, Betsy, and that is what he will always be. Of this I have absolutely no doubt whatsoever. He may well die in the line of duty. He may be dead as we speak, even."

Tears coursed down Betsy's cheeks again. Virginia continued, "Maybe he's still alive, of course, and I don't mean to alarm you, but if you marry him, every day for the rest of your life you will always wonder if he'll return home or not. Every day, Betsy. Often, he will not be there for you when you need him most. He'll be out hunting the vermin of the earth instead of in your bed or by your side. Your child will, for all intents, grow up fatherless. I know these things, Betsy, because my father was a soldier…almost as bad, if not worse, than a lawman. He died in the line of duty and it was over a year before my mother found out. It nearly broke her."

"So, do I just forget about him, Virginia? Live like a hermit here and raise my daughter alone?"

"You need not live like a hermit, Betsy. People talk, but soon someone else will cause a small scandal and your episode will fade."

"But what about my little girl? Will people accept her?"

"Betsy, by the time your daughter grows up, very few people will remember anything about her past. And besides, the way Prescott is booming, there'll be a whole new population here."

"It's hard for me to hear you say these things, Virginia. You know how much I love Jake."

"How much do you really know about Jake, Betsy?"

The girl paused, stumped momentarily. "Well, I know he grew up on a ranch and has a sister. Sophy. And some brothers." She chewed on her upper lip, trying to bring forth more facts about Jake.

"Jake is a complicated man, Betsy. Of course he never told you, but his first love was an Indian girl. A Cherokee girl. He intended to run off with her, but his father had the girl's entire village burned down and many of her people slaughtered." Virginia watched Betsy's eyes widen in shock.

CANYON OF DEATH

"That can't be true!"

"Yes, Betsy. It's quite shocking and unacceptable, considering that he came from a good family. But, I guess what I'm trying to say is that if he loved an Indian girl, is this the kind of man you want?"

"That doesn't matter, Virginia. It's in the past. I know Jake loves me as much – or more – as he did the other girl. I won't have you saying bad things about Jake. I won't!"

Virginia sighed. All right. Since that tactic wasn't going to work, she'd try a different approach. "Of course, dear. I'm sure you're right. But all I'm trying to say is that you don't really know Jake like you think you do. You're infatuated with him, Betsy. And that's understandable. He's a very attractive man. One that any woman would enjoy being with."

Virginia got up to close the window to give herself some thinking time. The conversation wasn't going as she'd hoped. "You know, Betsy, Sophy found herself in a family way by some flashy gambling man. Then she ran off to marry a different man in Arizona. That's the reason Jake left, you know, to go and get her."

"How do you know all this?" Betsy asked.

"Sophy is very straightforward with me when I ask her questions. Fortunately, she is now in love with a most respectable military man. Which goes to show that anything is possible, dear, and this is not the end of the world for you. I know there are plenty of men who wouldn't hesitate for even a moment to marry you, baby and all."

"Like who? I hardly know anyone. Living way out here has its limitations."

"Well, I can think of someone you know quite well who adores you in every way possible."

Betsy scrunched up her face, trying to imagine who the person could possibly be. "Who in the heck is that?" she finally asked.

"You really don't know?" Virginia laughed. "Gunner, dear. Gunner simply adores you."

"*Gunner?*"

"Don't tell me you haven't noticed his furtive looks, Betsy. And he dotes on the baby, too."

"Gunner…" Betsy said slowly, her mind awhirl. "No, Virginia, I can't marry Gunner."

"Pray tell, why not?"

"Well, I don't love him for one thing. I love Jake."

"Betsy, love is entirely over-rated. And, it's surprising how much one can fall in love after marriage. Love grows. The best course for a woman is to find a promising prospect and marry him. Love may or may not come, but at least the woman has a good spouse. One that stays at home and tends to business."

Betsy sat speechless, trying to assimilate what Virginia was saying.

"Gunner has fine qualities, Betsy. He's a hard worker, for one. He never complains, no matter how many chores are piled on him. He toils from morning until night. He's polite and honest. He's not a drinker or gambler, although most men do imbibe from time to time. I've sent him into town on many errands and he always does as bid with no deviation." Virginia paused, pleased with her argument. "I've even given him money to buy clothes that would fit him proper, but he won't take it. Says he can make do, that he doesn't feel right taking money when he's here just to help out."

"No matter what you say, Virginia, I won't marry Gunner. I just won't."

"I'm just asking you to think about these things, dear. It's not my intention to talk you into anything or to demean Jake Silver. But, and this is the last I'll say on the subject, Gunner would stay by your side always. He adores you, Betsy. He would be faithful and take good care of you and this property. He wouldn't be riding off in pursuit of trouble every time you turned around. Gunner would be there when you needed him. Besides, he's also a nice-looking young man. That never hurts, you know."

"Oh, Virginia. My head is spinning."

"You don't need to make any decisions today, dear. Or at all, for that matter." Virginia paused, then said, "Actually, you do need to make one decision."

"What's that?" Betsy asked.

"You need to give your daughter a name. She's two weeks old and doing well. In fact, I hear her fussing now. I'll go get her."

"Virginia? Will you move her bassinet in here? I'm…I'm ready to be her mother."

CANYON OF DEATH

***

Betsy thought long and hard about her conversation with Virginia. Much of what the woman said made sense, she hated to admit. But in her heart, she loved Jake and vowed she would never settle for someone else.

She did, however, begin to notice Gunner's glances. Twice she caught his eye, and the second time the two of them locked eyes for several moments. Betsy finally broke her gaze and looked down, blushing. When she looked up, Gunner still stood looking at her, his big brown eyes not hiding his longing or his love. He moved closer and gently touched her cheek. "I'm glad you're feeling better, Betsy," he said, then turned and left the room.

Her heart pounded and her face burned. What was she to make of this? Had Virginia talked to Gunner also? Was the woman attempting to be a matchmaker? Betsy would have to make a point of avoiding Gunner, lest he feel encouraged. Yet, his touch had been tender, and his warm, chocolate eyes had bathed her in love. Flustered, she stood, not certain which way to turn. Sophy, coming through the kitchen door, had seen the encounter, but hadn't said anything.

Christmas arrived, and the first snows fell, blanketing the ranch like a beautiful white quilt. There had been no word from Jake, and Betsy feared that Virginia's direful prediction of Jake's demise could be true. It had been well over two months since he'd left the Kaibito Tading Post, and she felt certain he would have sent a telegraph, or found some other way to reach her, if all was well. She alternately mourned his loss and cursed him for abandoning her. Nightly, she cried herself to sleep. She had to come to terms with it. Jake was gone.

Captain Burt, Sophy, Virginia, Gunner, and Betsy sat to Christmas dinner with a plump goose meticulously baked to perfection, one that Gunner had shot only days before. Virginia had decked the house with pine boughs, fancy store-bought decorations, and a trimmed tree, and despite her misery, Betsy joined in the festivities, trying her best to relish her baby's first Christmas.

At first, she'd tried to avoid looking at Gunner after her and Virginia's discussion, but that seemed impossible since she had the ranch to run and he was, essentially, there to do the work. No one suggested that maybe she should hire someone from town, and she ignored the idea when it popped into her head. She needed to talk with Gunner about paying him for his services, but she felt embarrassed to do so. She half feared he would tell her that he needed to return to Kaibito, yet she knew things could not continue on without a frank discussion.

Finally, at Christmas dinner, things began to come to a slow boil. Betsy sat at the head of the table, with Captain Burt and Sophy to her right, and Gunner and Virginia to her left. The baby sat propped in a chair between Betsy and Gunner. Aware of its meaning, no one mentioned the empty chair at the other end of the table, the place where Jake would have sat as head of the household.

"I'd like to propose a toast," said Captain Burt after plates were filled. He stood as he raised his glass, smiling at Sophy all the while. "I'd like to propose a toast to my beautiful fiancée, Sophia Silver." Shocked at the announcement, Betsy and Virginia sat momentarily with their mouths open before congratulating the couple. Only Gunner had the presence of mind to respond immediately.

"I proposed to Sophy a while back, but due to…." Burt paused and looked toward Jake's vacant seat. "Due to other considerations, we decided to postpone announcing our engagement until now."

"Congratulations!" Betsy said, still in shock. "You have given us the surprise of our lives. Sophy! I'm just…well, I'm just speechless."

Virginia also expressed her happiness for the couple, as did Gunner.

When Burt seated himself, Betsy stood, smiling nervously. "I, too, have an announcement to make." She received encouraging smiles, curiosity clearly written on every face.

"I would like to announce the name of my daughter. I know it's taken awhile," she said to the ensuing laughter. Nodding heads and eager faces awaited the pronouncement.

"Ladies and gentlemen, I'd like to introduce you to Margaret Marie. Named after my deceased mother, and my missing sister."

"Oh Betsy! That's a beautiful name," Virginia gushed.

"Yes! A perfect name," said Sophy. The men likewise nodded in approval.

"Here's to Margaret Marie Silver," said Burt, again raising his glass in toast.

"Hear, hear," came the response.

"No. She will take my maiden name. Her name is Margaret Marie DuBonnet. Not Silver," Betsy said, her impassive face saying what she could not, would not say. She alone raised her glass as Peter Burt, Sophy, and Virginia sat speechless. Only Gunner half raised his goblet in response.

Slowly the others raised their goblets, all except Captain Burt, who only looked at Betsy with grave concern. "Well," he said after an awkward pause, "let's eat, shall we? We shouldn't let this fine meal get cold."

Slowly, conversation revived, mostly regarding Sophy and Burt's plans for their wedding. Betsy guardedly did not look at Gunner, nor he her during the course of the meal. Only Margaret Marie uttered little baby squeals of delight as though pleased by her new name.

After dinner the small group gathered in the drawing room, sitting by the hearth and exchanging a few precious gifts. Betsy swallowed hard to control the lump in her throat when Burt presented his gift to Sophy, a beautiful shawl of the finest wool. Betsy had no gift from Jake, and her heart felt ready to break. And then, Gunner presented her with an extraordinarily lovely wood carving he'd fashioned. Caught off guard, she blushed, feeling grateful and pleased. An awkward silence followed as she placed the carving on the mantle.

Captain Burt, usually one to leave early, stayed on. Betsy watched the captain and Sophy with both envy and sadness in her heart – envy for Sophy's good fortune to be engaged, sadness for Jake's absence. Looking about and stifling her tears, she caught Gunner again watching her. She smiled at him briefly but looked away, conscious that he continued to openly, almost defiantly, gaze at her.

Finally, Burt rose to take his leave and Betsy saw him speak briefly to Gunner. She watched Gunner's face color, but he also stood and said good evening to the three women.

***

After a long hug and a respectable kiss, Burt left Sophy in the vestibule. Gunner awaited him on the snow-laden porch.

"When the weather permits, I'll be leaving to search for Jake," Burt said, looking directly at Gunner. "I didn't want to tell the women of my plans, as I don't want to get their hopes up and then possibly have them dashed."

"Good luck to you," Gunner responded.

"Jake is my friend, and of course Betsy is worried sick about him, as is Sophy."

Gunner nodded.

"So, it seems you'll be able to return home once I've found Jake and brought him back. It probably won't be long. I only tell you this so you won't think of getting too settled here."

"And what the hell is that supposed to mean?" Gunner retorted, his temper flaring.

"It means exactly what it sounds like. Don't be getting ideas about wooing Betsy. She's in a vulnerable position and might be easily taken advantage of. I saw you looking at her tonight in a way that suggests there's more to your feelings than merely being her ranch hand."

"Who the hell gives you the right to tell me what I can and cannot do?" Gunner stormed, stepping menacingly toward the much larger man. "I'm the one working here, working every damn day. Running this place, for all practical purposes."

"Listen, son, I'm telling you this for your own good. Jake will return, and he will claim Betsy."

"Yeah? And what if she don't want him no more?"

"Jake will have his way, Gunner. One way or another. He loves her, and he won't take no for an answer."

Gunner stood silent a moment. "Well, he could be dead, you know."

"I suppose that's possible, but my gut feeling tells me he isn't."

The two men walked down the steps toward the barn where Burt's horse awaited and where Gunner lived in Thomas Jefferson's quarters.

"Tell you what, *Captain*," Gunner said with a sneer as they approached the barn. "You keep your orders for men who are stupid enough to follow you. I'm the man around here. I won't harbor you giving me orders or advice again."

CANYON OF DEATH

Burt flinched but did not reach out and grab the young man. Maybe Jake was dead. Maybe he wasn't. But Burt knew now he would do everything in his power to keep Betsy from marrying Gunner.

WINTER IN THE CHIRICAHUAS

As Nantan Lupan foretold, for three days after his departure the skies remained cheerily blue. On the fourth day heavy clouds moved in, and late in the day a blizzard struck. Jake hoped that Nantan Lupan and Tiponi had traveled well out of the area, or at least had found a safe place to weather the storm. The Indian was a survivor, though, so Jake didn't worry too much.

Under Emma and Neil's care, Jake's condition improved daily in the following weeks, but not enough to mount up and return to Prescott. Had he been able to do so, the weather would have prevented it, anyway. Storm after storm blew through the area, leaving snow piled high around the cabin.

Despite the tight quarters, not a day passed without merriment in the household. Emma prepared incredibly delicious meals from almost nothing, it seemed. While watching the woman putter and fuss about the kitchen and Neil work on their home, Jake saw true happiness, the happiness that comes from a couple with shared ideas and dreams and who were not afraid of hard work. He realized he didn't have this with Betsy. Shocked at the realization, he put it out of his mind.

He wondered if he now had a son or daughter. "I don't care which it is," he commented to Emma one day. "On balance, I'd say life is harder for a woman, so maybe it'd be better if it's a boy." After he said it, he recognized that life wouldn't be hard for any child of Betsy's, what with Betsy's inheritance. Still, women seemed more fragile and delicate, so perhaps a boy would be best.

Neil fashioned Jake a pair of crutches, and it wasn't long before he stood. "How long should the splint stay on?" Jake asked.

"That, my dear friend, is a mighty fine question. I haven't any idea. I'll ask the doctor the next time I go to town or to the fort. He may want to see you before he gives an opinion."

That sounded good to Jake, who was developing a serious case of cabin fever. All his wounds were healing nicely, some even completely closed and scabbed over, thanks to Emma's ministrations. Only the leg remained a problem.

Within a week, however, Jake was hobbling a few steps around the cabin on the crutches. He sat at the table for meals. He would've walked more, but the small, two-room cabin didn't have space to roam. He wanted to put pressure on the leg, but hesitated lest he cause it pain or make it worse.

A month later, Jake and Neil took a sleigh to Fort Bowie where the attending physician pronounced, after some painful prodding and poking, that the leg must remain splinted for another month. Downhearted at the news, Jake nevertheless took a short, laborious trek on his crutches down the cleared boardwalks, enjoying the fresh air and being out amongst people, while Neil attended to business. He and Neil would stay over and return to the Chiricahua cabin in the morning, the distance being too far to make a round trip in the heavy, snowy conditions. As he prepared to hobble back to the sleeping quarters he and Neil had been assigned, a man deliberately stepped in front of his path, blocking the way. Glancing up, Jake saw Peter Burt standing before him.

"Peter!"

"Jake! What in the hell happened to you?" Burt asked. "You look godawful."

"Thanks," Jake said, smiling at his friend. "What are you doing here?"

"Looking for you. Let's go somewhere we can talk," Burt suggested, guiding Jake to a local establishment.

The two men entered the fort's only saloon, took a table, and ordered coffee. The first drink of the dark bitter brew tasted heavenly. "Haven't had a good cup of coffee since I don't remember when. Emma Erickson serves only tea," he said, savoring the aroma and taste.

"Tell me. What's gone on?" Burt, all business, dispensed with the small talk.

"Got shot up real bad. Didn't think I'd make it. You remember our friend, Nantan Lupan?"

Burt nodded. "Yes, the Indian who kidnapped Sophy, and whom we let live for some ridiculous reason."

"Well, that Apache came to my rescue. If it hadn't been for him, I'd be lying dead in that canyon of death instead of six other men. Got shot in the back by a renegade, then the hooligans opened fire on me." Jake involuntarily shuddered thinking about it. "I did, however, manage to kill Johnny Geiger."

"So, was it worth it?" Burt asked, a seriousness in his demeanor.

"What do you mean? Of course it was worth it. I got the bastard that kidnapped Betsy and beat her senseless."

"And you, my friend, have little else."

"What's that supposed to mean?"

"It means, that when I left Prescott to come look for you, you were in the process of losing Betsy to the young man from Kaibito. Gunner."

"Gunner? He's just a kid," Jake scoffed, remembering the dark-haired, slender young man.

"Not such a kid, Jake. He's been running the ranch in your absence. He may be younger than you, but he's older than Betsy, and becoming quite a capable ranch hand."

"Well, what about Thomas Jefferson?"

"According to Virginia Hall, Jefferson died shortly after you left on your manhunt."

"I didn't know," Jake said, stunned by the news. After a pause, he asked, "So what's really going on?"

"What's going on is that Gunner is devotedly, upside down in love with Betsy. The feeling is not yet reciprocated, but things will likely come to a head soon enough. The kid can't be left in limbo forever. He'll become more aggressive and force her decision, I'm sure," Burt paused a moment. "She is, after all, in a tough spot."

Jake sat, staring into the dregs of his cup. Finally, he said, "Well, I've been holed up all winter recovering from bullet holes and a broken leg. I'm stuck in this damn splint for another month, according to the doctor here."

"Jake, what's wrong with you? Time was, you'd have gone through hell to get to Betsy. Now, what're you doing? You're hiding out in the Chiricahuas."

Angry at the insinuation, Jake held his retort. Was Burt right? *Was* he just stalling? "I'm not hiding out! I don't know. I've had thoughts that maybe I'm not right for her."

Burt scoffed, then said, "Did you know you're the father of a little girl?"

"A girl? Does she look like Betsy?"

"Who'd want your ugly mug?" Burt teased. "She looks like her mother all right. Betsy named her Margaret Marie."

"Sure, after her mother and sister. A fine name."

"Yes, except it's Margaret Marie DuBonnet."

Jake said nothing, but fully understood the extent of Betsy's fury with him.

"You'd best get back, Jake. The sooner the better, or it's over for the two of you. Betsy will marry Gunner, if she hasn't already."

"I – I had no idea things would come to something like this," Jake finally responded.

"Believe it." Burt took a sip of coffee and then continued. "I asked Sophy to marry me, by the way. Right before Christmas. She said yes. Wanted you to know."

"That's good. That's real good, Peter. I wish you all the luck and happiness in the world."

"Where are you staying?"

"I'm out at Neil and Emma Ericksons' place. Been there since Nantan Lupan brought me in."

"I'll stop by after I check out this canyon with all the dead bodies in it. Rucker's Canyon, right?" Burt asked. "Heard someone talking about coming across some dead bodies down that way. Probably should retrieve what's left of the remains – or bury them. If you're up to it and ready when I come by, you can ride back with us. But at least now I can tell everyone you're alive and report what happened. That might help your situation."

Both men stood and shook hands. "Well, I'd better be getting back to the lodging. Neil will be wondering what happened to me," Jake said. "Thanks, Peter. I'll be mounted and waiting when you come back through."

Jake hobbled out the door, more on his mind that he knew what to do with. He considered briefly of writing to Betsy, but then thought better of it, knowing he could be more persuasive in person. Maybe a telegram? More dramatic, perhaps. Instead of doing either, he brooded.

Unlike the ride to the fort where Jake had chatted amiably, on the journey back he remained taciturn and withdrawn. He had a lot of thinking to do. He couldn't bring himself to picture Betsy and Gunner together, but he certainly hadn't been there with her, or for her, for some months. *Why not Gunner?* he asked himself. He was a good kid. Still, it galled him to think that someone had taken his place so quickly. He'd only been gone a few months. Four, plus the time he'd spent looking for Sophy. It was early February now. He wondered when he could head back.

He no sooner asked the question than he realized it would be best to take Burt up on his offer and return to Prescott when the captain did. Traveling in the winter alone could be dicey. That meant he must start using his leg right away. Walking. Riding.

He removed the splint the next morning, ignoring Neil's admonishments and Emma's worries. "I gotta get back to Prescott," he said. "It's urgent." He didn't want to explain his predicament, so he avoided their questions and ignored their concerns.

His leg, weak after being immobile for so long, hurt like hell when he tried to stand on it. Maybe it wouldn't be so bad when he rode, he hoped. There'd be little weight on it, although once in the saddle, the leg would be bent at the knee for long hours at a time. Determined not to give up, he started off by standing on it for a few minutes at a time, two dozen times a day for a few days, and massaged it after each attempt. After three days he took a few steps, wincing with each one. He felt inclined to limp, but moved slowly so he wouldn't. He used the crutches to walk, cautiously putting more weight on the leg when he thought it seemed ready to bear it.

At first, he felt confident walking with assistance at a snail's pace back and forth in the cabin. Soon he discarded the crutches and hobbled without assistance. He did this repeatedly, with a short rest between each sojourn to the opposite wall. At night his leg ached, but he refrained from using the laudanum.

CANYON OF DEATH

Snow continued to fall off and on over the next two weeks, and there was no sign of Peter Burt. Instead of the snow being beautiful, it now seemed more like a warden, keeping him incarcerated. But he felt more confident with each passing day and found himself hoping that Burt would hold off just a bit longer so he'd be able to make the trip. He finally ventured outdoors, painfully navigating the porch steps, and crossed the snowy yard to the barn where Wild Bill greeted him with the most obnoxious series of brays he'd yet heard.

"Yeah. It's me, Bill. I haven't forgotten you," Jake said, scratching the mule's furry forehead. It didn't look like the mule had fared too poorly over the winter, judging by the bulging belly that swayed and jiggled when the animal walked. "Looks like you've been well fed, buddy. We'll have to walk some of that off you."

Unlike Wild Bill, Jake could tell he'd lost weight. His britches hung on his hips, and his face looked thinner and strained from the constant pain. He found himself easily exhausted, also, something he'd never experienced before. But then again, he consoled himself, he'd never been shot up and at death's door before, either.

But as the days passed, he began to feel notable improvement in his well-being. He split firewood, fed the animals, and hauled water regularly for Emma, relieving Neil of some of the more tedious, time-consuming chores. After a full day of moving about, his leg often ached unmercifully, though.

"Best move yourself out to California," Neil commented one night after supper. "Weather there's a bit milder. I think it's easier on the bones and joints. So I've heard."

"Not a bad idea," Jake said. I'd like to see the ocean someday, anyhow."

"Yah. That's goot. I've seen the ocean. Not the Pacific, but the Atlantic. Crossed it, I did," Neil said, getting excited and reverting to an accent.

Jake sat, imagining Neil on a boat big enough to cross an ocean. "What was it like?"

"Mighty scary at times, I must admit. I got a wee bit seasick, I did. Still, there was a lot of beauty in it," Neil said, a dreamy look on his face. "Very magical how the wind can both push and pull a boat along. I never quite figured out how that works. But no matter the wind direction, the boat pretty much sails the way it's steered. I come from a seafaring country, but my folks never ventured out on a boat."

"Hmm. I can't picture a body of water that big."

"So big it took us over a month to sail across it. Sailed day and night. Nonstop."

"Well – I…." Jake wanted to say that maybe someday he would cross an ocean, but that seemed out of the question if he married Betsy. He'd probably end up being a rancher like his father had been. He figured his law days most likely would be over by the time he got to Prescott, considering how long he'd been gone.

"What brought you to this country, Neil? If you don't mind my asking."

Neil puffed on his pipe. "I come for revenge. That's always a bad beginning. I know that now. My father, you see, came before me and was killed by Indians. When word filtered back, I vowed to come and avenge his death by killing as many Indians as I could. I joined the military two days after landing, though I barely spoke English." He stopped and relit the pipe. "It didn't take me more than a year or two, though, to see things a mite differently. I came to learn quite a bit about the red man, and I could see that he'd been unfairly treated, and cheated, by whites. After a bit, I began to have some sympathy for the native folk. Not too much, and not that I ever forgave them for killing me pa, but I lost my bloodlust. Met Emma, and once I got out of the military, we married and moved here. Beautiful piece of land. I can see why the Indians fought so to hold onto it."

Jake nodded in understanding and began cleaning and oiling his guns again, especially the Colts which had been exposed to sand and grit.

"So, when you plannin' on leavin' us, Jake?" Neil asked, tapping the tobacco from his pipe.

"I'm hoping to go with Captain Burt when he returns from the canyons. He's investigating the shooting down there, I guess. Not sure what's happened to him."

"That could be a spell. Maybe they be having bigger snows on that side of the mountains than here."

"I suppose that's good, in a way, although I'd like to get back. See my daughter before she's all grown up," Jake said, smiling.

CANYON OF DEATH

The following day Jake saddled Wild Bill for the first time. Nantan Lupan did not ride in a saddle, and he'd left Jake's saddle, bridle, and other gear. "Bet that stubborn Indian is sorry he didn't have this bridle and bit," Jake muttered, picturing the small man trying to control the headstrong stud. But now, he couldn't believe he, Jake Silver, U.S. Deputy Marshal, was going to ride a mule back to Prescott. Mules had been used strictly as beasts of burden on his father's ranch. He knew them to be smart and strong, but thought them certainly no match for a horse.

Hesitant to mount, but knowing the day of reckoning would soon be at hand, he mounted the mule from the opposite side, to spare his left leg the pain of bearing his full weight when he swung into the saddle. Expecting the mule to rebel from the odd-side mounting, he kept a firm grip on the reins, but Wild Bill stood calmly.

Moving out of the barn, Jake headed the animal up a path packed firmly by Neil's frequent passage to the woodpile, and was astonished at how fast the mule walked out. Even on unpacked snow, the mule did not slow. He returned from the ride an hour later amazed at the animal's rigor and smooth gait.

Jake began to think about leaving without Burt. Burt's mount probably wouldn't be able to keep up with the mule's gait, anyway, he realized. Another big snowfall postponed his plan, however. Fighting off impatience to depart, Jake used the time to check, and recheck, his guns, strengthen his leg, and practice walking without a limp.

The first of March arrived before the weather warmed enough that winter gave signs of waning. "I think I'll be on my way in the next day or two," Jake said one evening.

"Yah. I figure you be heading home soon. You won't be waiting for your friend, then?"

"No. If he comes along, tell him I've left."

"I think you best be takin' this with you, Jake." Neil held out the tin badge Jake had given him months before. "We have no need of it. You do."

As Jake studied the badge, a mountain of thoughts and emotions overwhelmed him. The badge meant so much to him, but it had cost him too much. But who was he, really, without it? Just another drifter. The badge gave him meaning, at least for now.

"Thank you, Neil. I reckon I would like to have that back. It was good of you to keep it for me, and to think of it now," Jake said, taking the star and tucking it into his shirt pocket. "If I still got a job, I'll be wearing it proudly." He almost added, *and if my girl won't mind me wearing it,* but the words stuck in his craw.

That night he gathered his few belongings and prepared for the upcoming journey. Thoughts of Betsy swept through him. Maybe she'd be married to Gunner by now, and if so, his being a marshal wouldn't be an issue. One minute he realized that her marrying Gunner might be the best thing for both of them, but the next minute he couldn't imagine never holding her in his arms again. Never making love to her, never seeing her blonde hair shimmer in the sun, or her smile light up her whole face. The merriment of her laughter teased his ears. He had a daughter to think of now, too, and Betsy couldn't just take his fatherhood away from him.

He hardly slept, anxious to begin the journey. But when morning came, he realized he'd miss the kind people who'd kept him all winter and had nursed him back to health and good humor with their attention. He'd found it painfully difficult to say goodbye to Nantan Lupan, and it'd be just as difficult to say goodbye to Neil and Emma, who had literally saved him from death's beck and call.

The three stood awkwardly, everybody a bit teary-eyed. Emma had packed Jake enough food and supplies to last a week at the very least. Neil gave him an extra bedroll and more cartridges, along with a heavy wool coat.

"Don't know how I can repay you folks," Jake said. "I have some money on me, and I can give you half of it now. I'll send you more as soon as I get back. I got plenty in an account in Prescott. I'd like to return this summer and help some more with the house, too," he added. "I'd like to bring Betsy and Margaret Marie with me."

"That would be payment enough, Jake. We're not needing money, but we can always use a worker with a good strong back," Neil said. "You keep your funds in your pocket, and I think you best not be sleeping out on the ground. Stay in hotels and inns or way stations. You'll be safer, and your leg will thank you."

"Oh, I do hope you can return, Jake," Emma said, wiping away tears. "I'd love some female companionship around here. It'd be so wonderful to see you again, too."

"I'll let you know when I'm coming. You can count on it," Jake said, firmly shaking hands with Neil, Emma squashing him in a bear hug.

Mounting Wild Bill, Jake waved and the mule took off at a rapid clip. "Best spare yourself, Bill. We got a lot of miles ahead of us," Jake admonished the animal. But the mule kept on, the day warmed, and Jake rejoiced that he was, at long last, going home.

A DECISION

Prescott's frigid winter slowly wound down, and spring arrived quickly. Cows began dropping their calves, and Gunner hastily learned how to pull a calf when necessary. His help on the ranch had become indispensible, and everyone knew it, though no one mentioned it.

Virginia Hall moved back to her boarding house after the holidays. Even though her hired girl ran the rooming house with the same meticulous attention and care that Virginia herself did, Virginia decided she should leave, especially since Sophy now stayed at the ranch house. She came to call frequently, however, and became like a grandmother to little Maggie, the name most everyone now called Margaret Marie.

Betsy had her hands full. Each year her herd had grown, and new colts had come along, too. What with the continuous maintenance on the property, she contemplated hiring a seasonal hand. Gunner worked all day, every day, and could barely keep up with the demands of the growing ranch. She half feared Gunner would leave someday, and she knew what she had to do to keep him there.

He'd been eating his meals with her and Sophy, just as Thomas Jefferson had, but he'd taken up residence in the sleeping quarters in the barn. Despite Virginia's counsel, Betsy had no idea of the true extent of Gunner's infatuation with her. She didn't understand that he thought of her continuously, and looked for her throughout the day. Nor did she realize that mealtimes were the highlight of his days when he sat across from her and stole lovesick glances. She knew he found her attractive, but she underestimated to what extreme his attraction to her had grown. Often she joined him in the chores, having no idea that he could hardly bear to have her so near for so long without holding her in his arms.

Betsy endeavored to avoid direct eye contact with Gunner, hoping to steer clear of any situation which might encourage him. Yet, she herself stole many glances at him and had begun to admire his growing manly appearance physical labor had brought about.

She missed Jake terribly, but she'd come to the heartbreaking conclusion that he'd been killed by Johnny Geiger, or some renegade or desperado, and lay dead somewhere in the Chiricahua wilderness. She craved his touch, his arms about her, the security she felt when he was around. She awoke at night, deeply yearning for him, but his side of the bed remained cold and empty. How much longer could she wait for him? She would lie in bed thinking of him, crying and praying for his return.

Other times she felt the deepest hatred for the man who'd left her when she'd needed him most, who had changed the course of her entire life, and she half-hoped he *had* died. It would serve him right, but then she'd quickly recant and regret her thoughts.

She would decide what to do soon. Gunner was there and available, and she was an unwed mother. Despite her fortune, she had a questionable reputation, money or no money, that she suspected most men would have difficulty overlooking. Gunner, like Jake, didn't seem to be impressed with her inheritance, or even care about it. Virginia had told her that Gunner loved her, and he'd confirmed that in many small ways. She also knew she could make him love her even more.

Wisely, Sophy never commented on Betsy's personal life. The two women gave each other a wide berth and much latitude. Betsy knew that Sophy herself had experienced her fair share of woes, yet despite all that she was now engaged to Captain Peter Burt, a respectable, handsome, intelligent man. Betsy wondered if she would ever be so fortunate. Perhaps Gunner was not a bad choice.

Fortunately, Margaret Marie kept Betsy occupied and happy and from making any immediate decisions. Already crawling and climbing, the tiny child could move faster than a skittish filly, and the mischievous tyke kept Betsy and Sophy on their toes. Several times they'd found the baby crawling under the pasture fence, and twice Gunner had brought the child back from her unexpected visit to the barn.

Gunner's fondness of the child was apparent to anyone who saw the two together.

A decision would have to be made.

"Sophy, have you heard anything from Peter?" Betsy asked when Sophy returned from town one afternoon.

Sophy shook her head. "Not yet." She smiled sadly at Betsy. "Don't give up hope, Betsy."

"I can't wait forever. It's been months and months."

"You're thinking, then, about taking up with Gunner?"

Betsy nodded and looked away.

"Betsy, Gunner is a good man. He loves you. Anyone can see that. I love my brother, but honestly, I think he'd understand, given your circumstances. But don't do this unless you're absolutely sure. Don't hurt Gunner or yourself," *or Jake*, it was clear she wanted to add but didn't.

"But what if he's alive, Sophy? How can I marry Gunner, not knowing? I'll never love Gunner as much as I love Jake," Betsy cried.

"I understand that, too. Believe me. Before Peter, I was madly in love with a man for years. It was his child I lost, in fact. I love Peter, but it's a different kind of love than I had before. I think a woman's first love leaves an indelible mark on her. It can never be repeated, but that doesn't mean I don't love Peter. It's just – well, it's just different, that's all. Not worse."

"Would you go back to that first man if he came back into your life?" Betsy asked.

Sophy paused, deep in thought. "No, Betsy. I've learned some hard lessons since then – and because of him, I might also add. Even though I often think of him and wonder what he's doing, I could never go back. I guess I know too much now. There's more to love than that addictive, wildly passionate lovemaking. That's really all we had. I'm not saying it wasn't wonderful and superb and irresistible, but there's more to love than that, and I've found it in Peter. Peter is steady, gentle, good, and kind. He makes me laugh. I know he loves me."

Betsy nodded in understanding. Is physical passion all she had with Jake? The question hit her hard. She loved the smell of him, the feel of him. It's true she desperately missed their intimacy, but she was hard pressed to come up with other feelings they shared. Except he made her laugh, and feel safe. Wasn't that enough?

The afternoon passed, and soon Gunner came in for the evening meal.

"Good evening, Gunner. How were things in the field today?" Betsy asked. "Any new calves?" She could tell by the look on his face that her greeting and question surprised him. She smiled warmly at him. "I made your favorite dessert for tonight, so leave some room for it."

Another wave of surprise passed over his visage, but he merely nodded and smiled happily in response.

Betsy chatted gaily while the three of them ate. "Gunner, could you drive me into town tomorrow?" she asked. "I have business I'd like to attend to. If you don't mind, that is. I won't take too long."

Everyone knew Betsy to be perfectly capable of driving herself to town, or even riding for that matter. Both women watched Gunner's face as he responded.

"I guess I could do that. I got some more fencing to repair, but I suppose that could wait a day," Gunner finally said, smiling.

"Wonderful. What time would you like me to be ready?"

"Let's leave early. That way I can maybe get some work done in the afternoon."

"Perfect. Sophy, would you mind the baby for me tomorrow?"

***

Gunner helped Betsy into the wagon, still somewhat surprised at her sudden change of tone and exaggerated friendliness. He slapped the reins and the horse began to move. He noticed that Betsy sat a bit closer than expected, but he figured it was unintentional on her part.

She chatted amiably, talking of the baby, the ranch, Sophy's upcoming nuptials. She even solicited his opinion about a horse she'd looked at with the idea of using the animal as a herd stud for a year or two, since Jake had taken off with the stud she'd planned to use.

Caught off guard, Gunner grew quiet, uneasy about the sudden change in Betsy. While he wanted to enjoy her undivided attention, he sensed a huge boulder preparing to fall on him. Maybe she was getting ready to fire him and was just being nice because she felt bad about it. A mile out of Prescott, Gunner brought the wagon to a halt.

"Is something wrong?" Betsy asked.

"Yes, Betsy. Something's wrong. This is wrong. What's going on? Why are we here together? You. Me."

Betsy looked down, bashful, sweet, and innocent. "You're right, Gunner. I should apologize."

"For what?"

"Gunner, I've been unfair to you. I've ignored my feelings for so long. You've been so good to me, from the very first day, and I've treated you indifferently, even though that's not how I've felt about you."

When he didn't respond, she gamely continued. "I've grown to care for you, Gunner. I just haven't known how to show it, and it's been very awkward, what with me giving birth to another man's baby and all. I knew you couldn't possibly care for me in return, even though you've been so gentle and sweet to me. I just couldn't bear your rebuff. I just wanted to spend some time with you. I've wanted to do so for so long, Gunner, so I made up an excuse today. I hope you'll forgive me and not think me forward." She dabbed a hanky to her dry eyes.

Gunner's face burned. He'd dreamed of something like this, and now it was happening. Surprised into silence, he sat for a moment, rubbing the leather reins with this thumbs. "Betsy, I don't know what to say."

"Just don't say you hate me for this. I couldn't bear it!"

He looked at the young woman beside him, tongue tied. He adored her and thought of her endlessly every moment of every waking day, but dare he believe her now?

"Betsy," he began. "Just tell me the truth. Are you doing this to spite Jake, or because you think he might be dead?"

"Gunner, Jake died to me that day at the Kaibito Trading Post when he refused to stay with me. He preferred to go chasing after Johnny Geiger instead of staying with the stranded, beaten woman who was about to bear his child and who desperately needed him. When I thought about it, I realized it had always been that way with Jake. He took no interest in the ranch. His only interest was in me – in bed. I'm ashamed to say this. Deeply ashamed. It took my kidnapping and beating for me to realize Jake only cared about the tin badge he wore and about riding around the countryside. I have not loved him since that day. It was a rude awakening. And now I've spoken out of turn," she said, this time a tiny trickle of tears flowing.

"If you love me, Betsy, truly love me, then you need to marry me or I'll leave. I can't take any more watching you and not, well, not having you as my wife."

"Is that an ultimatum, Gunner?"

"I hadn't thought of it that way, but I suppose it is. I ache with longing for you, Betsy. I love you. I love Maggie. I love you more than I ever imagined it possible to love anyone," Gunner said with heartbreaking sincerity. "Now I've spoken my piece. The rest is up to you. It's your decision, but I hope you make your mind up fast. I can't take any more of this."

Betsy threw her arms about him. "Oh, Gunner! Honestly, you want to marry me? I'm so thrilled! And surprised. Yes! Yes! I'll marry you!"

"Shall we visit the Justice of the Peace while we're in town?" Gunner asked. Though smiling broadly, he couldn't quite believe this fortunate turn of events.

Betsy hesitated a moment. "Gunner, I'd like to be married in my home. *Our* home now. Can we wait until after Easter? It's only a bit more than a month."

Disappointment flooded him.

Quickly Betsy went on, "I've never been married before, Gunner. I'd like it to be special. I need to make a dress. And wouldn't you like to invite your parents? I want Virginia to come, and Peter Burt."

She looked so earnest and adorable, Gunner couldn't say no, even though the date would be an excruciatingly long, six weeks away.

"Okay. Easter."

"No, silly. The week after."

"Right." He looked at Betsy, dying to hold her in his arms. "Betsy, may I kiss you?"

She moved closer, and Gunner pulled her onto his lap. The kiss was more passionate than he'd thought he could get away with, but Betsy's response urged him on, and soon he had to gently push her away lest he lose all control. "It's going to be a long six weeks," he commented as she settled herself.

Upon entering town, Betsy's posturing made it clear that she and Gunner were now a couple. Tongues clucked as she held his arm and walked about town. She smiled adoringly at him, even giving him a peck on the cheek once. Gunner's happiness was only marred by a twinge of disbelief that dogged him.

The announcement of Betsy and Gunner's engagement surprised few who knew them. Others secretly agreed that Betsy was marrying Gunner in desperation to give her child legitimacy. It was also a fact that once Sophy married and left the ranch, it would be most inappropriate for Gunner to stay on with no chaperone present. No one wanted to see Betsy bear another illegitimate child, so no one openly criticized her decision, but many a coffee klatch relished the topic.

Sophy withheld any comment other than offering her congratulations. Even Virginia Hall, though she had once urged Betsy to consider Gunner as a prospective husband, now harbored second thoughts. Nevertheless, the couple planned their wedding. Betsy spent so much time keeping herself busy that she often missed mealtimes, leaving Gunner and Sophy to dine alone. Neither of them discussed the upcoming nuptials.

The weeks passed, and Gunner began to think that perhaps Betsy would actually marry him. His mother, Tilly, came from Kaibito early and insisted that he be outfitted appropriately. He could tell that she sensed an uneasiness in the relationship between him and Betsy, and he felt thankful that she kept her comments to herself and didn't question Betsy's motivation for marrying him. Knowing his mother, he knew she probably thought he and Betsy were not suited for each other. He wasn't Jake – that's what it all boiled down to in her eyes.

Despite Gunner's attempted caresses and kisses, Betsy steadfastly refused him any early marital privileges.

***

Three weeks before Betsy's wedding, Sophy ran from the carriage and burst through the door. "Betsy! Betsy! Come quickly!" Her hands shook as she held the letter from Peter Burt.

CANYON OF DEATH

"What, Sophy! What is it?" Betsy said, alarmed at Sophy's wild-eyed look and shaking hands.

"Oh, Betsy." Sophy looked at her with a mixture of sorrow and guilt. "Betsy, I just got a letter from Peter. Jake is alive, Betsy! He's alive!"

Betsy sat perfectly still, her face blanching.

"He's alive! He got all shot up and has been recovering in a cabin in the Chiricahuas for months. His leg is broken and everything, but he's recovering and on his way back! Isn't that wonderful?"

It took a half a minute before Betsy could speak. She sat there dumbfounded, thrilled, yet paralyzed with shock. Alive? After all this time? "That's such – good news, Sophy. I'm glad. Truly. You…" But she couldn't finish her statement. Tears gushed and she ran to her room, not caring that her sobs could plainly be heard throughout the house.

***

Gunner had watched Sophy's carriage travel much too fast down the drive, her leap from it and race into the house. She hadn't even bothered to secure the horse. He now hurried through the front door to discover the cause of the commotion and heard Besty's hysterical cries. "What the hell has happened?" he asked, starting up the stairs. Only Sophy's hand firmly latching onto him slowed him.

"Gunner, you'd best give her a moment. She's okay. She'll be okay. She's just had quite a shock. I should have presented the news differently," Sophy said. "I was just so excited and happy I wasn't thinking."

"Well, what the hell is so exciting and happy that she's up there bawlin' her eyes out about?"

"Gunner, Jake is alive," Sophy said softly.

"What?"

"Jake's alive. He got shot a bunch of times and broke his leg, but he's alive and coming home. It's all here in Peter's letter."

Gunner stood, silent a moment, before turning and walking to the front door. "This isn't his home, Sophy. Not anymore. I don't want him here," he said, anger coursing through him. "Betsy's not his girl anymore. She's mine. And we're gettin' married, and he ain't gonna interfere. He's already hurt her enough."

Tilly entered from the kitchen in time to hear her son speak.

"You can't demand that she love you, Gunner," Sophy said. "Maybe Betsy will marry you, and maybe she won't. But you can't demand it. It's her decision. I know she cares for you, Gunner," Sophy added, trying to soften the blow she knew would inevitably come. "But she also cares for Jake. She has his child."

"That bastard left her, and he'll leave her again. I'll never leave her," Gunner said, slamming out the door.

Tilly shook her head sadly. "I feared this from the start, and feared what would come of it," she sighed.

Upstairs, Betsy's wails continued.

HEADING HOME

A few miles from the cabin, Jake stopped and looked back at the Chiricahuas, standing glorious and mysterious, the peaks still snowcapped. It was a place he both loved and hated. He carried away with him many fond memories of his time with Nantan Lupan and the Ericksons, but he also carried away ugly scars and a leg that might never fully recover. Though he tried to shut out the memory of the shootout, it often slammed into him, causing him to cringe as he remembered the pain of the bullet piercing his back and the cavalcade of bullets that had narrowly missed him. The only good part of the whole horrible experience was seeing the surprised expression on Johnny Geiger's face when Jake pulled the trigger and shot him dead center of his forehead. Even that, however, contained a haunting element to it. Jake had killed men before in the line of duty, but never in hatred or for revenge. He'd gunned down a small handful of men for reasons even he didn't fully comprehend, but even then the men were outlaws and would've swung if they'd stood trial. The killing of Geiger had been different. It'd been personal.

Since both he and Wild Bill were not in the best of physical condition, Jake elected to make his first day a short one. He planned to stop in Dos Cabezas for the night. He didn't want to make camp given the weather, but he worried that if he stayed in the mining hamlet there'd be trouble if anyone recognized him as a lawman. Jake's reputation preceded him, and he enjoyed wide recognition throughout the territory, but that had its drawbacks, also. Fortunately, he saw a small structure a ways off the trail. Smoke wafted from the chimney, and the place had the look of a hardworking homesteaded outfit. Construction on fences was well underway, and clearing of cacti and brush was evident. It didn't look like an outlaw hideout. Still, he approached cautiously, hoping that the inhabitants would be friendly and maybe willing to accept a quarter or half-dollar to let him sleep in the lean-to with the mule.

The residents, a couple from Missouri who'd migrated West, welcomed him warmly. "It'll be good to have company for a spell," said the man who'd introduced himself as Walker Hanson. "My wife gets a bit lonesome out here. We don't see too many folk, and the Dos Cabezas residents are a little too rowdy for her."

"I'm obliged," Jake said, dismounting. "I'll put my mule up in your shed, if it's all the same to you."

"I'll accompany you, Marshal," Walker Hanson said. Without waiting for a response the man grabbed his coat.

"How'd you know I'm a marshal?" Jake asked.

"Word gets around." Walker said. "I heard plenty about you. Good things, mostly, and that's a comfort. I heard you killed six men over there in the Chiricahuas and got shot up a bit yourself,"

"Something like that. I had help, though. Friend of mine was along. Saved my life. Where'd you hear all this stuff, anyway?"

"I go to the fort periodically, and I heard some men talkin' about it. Seems you'd been in to see the doc and somehow the story got out. Heard you shot Johnny Geiger, even after you'd been shot in the back and was lyin' on the ground all busted up," Walker was clearly eager for details.

"That's a fact," Jake responded, not really wanting to discuss the incident. "Now, you got a good corral for the mule. I don't want to see him stolen during the night," Jake said, trying to change the subject.

"I'd say not. That's a fine animal there. A bit heavy, but a good-lookin' animal. Where'd you get him, if I may ask?"

"He's on loan. From a friend," Jake answered.

"You got some damn good friends, I'd say. My wife Mable and me used to raise mules back in Missouri. Did real good at it. Mules are in high demand," Walker said.

"Why'd you quit? Seems like you had a good thing going."

"Oh, we did all right. But we had differences of opinion with our fellow Missourians regarding political views. Been a feud goin' on between my family and the Haggertys for so long nobody rightly remembers the cause of it. Still, after a bunch of my cousins got shot up, the Haggertys come after our mules and shot a bunch of them up. Tryin' to chase us out, I guess. I just got discouraged," Walker said, a note of bitterness in his voice. "I always wanted to come out West anyway. I brought a couple mules with me, and I've sold 'em for a damn good profit. Plan on raisin' 'em here once we get settled in. Hope the move wasn't a mistake. The missus is all nervous now that she's heard about this here 'high country killer.' I figured maybe that's why you was here. I told her this wasn't particularly high country and not to fret, but you know what worriers women can be."

When no response came, Walker continued. "Got a nice little molly still, but my wife refuses to let me sell her."

"Yeah. I know how it goes when you get attached to an animal. I try not to," Jake said.

"You keep that mule long enough, Marshal, and you won't want to part with 'im."

"We'll see about that," Jake said.

With Wild Bill established in the shed with a serving of hay for two, the men returned to the house. Mabella Hanson fussed over her company, insisting that her stew was not salty enough and needed more fixins, and that the bread came out too dry and on and on. Jake complimented her after every bite, but it seemed the woman worried endlessly that her company wouldn't be pleased. "If I'd a known you were comin', Marshal, I'd a had Walker butcher us a chicken. Roasted chicken is my specialty," she said.

Fortunately, the Hansons were not late-night folks, so after Jake checked on Wild Bill, he laid down on the bedding Mrs. Hanson had made up for him on the floor in front of the hearth. His curiosity had been piqued by the mention of a high country killer, but he'd pointedly ignored the reference, and now he wondered what all it concerned, but he didn't feel inquisitive enough to pursue the topic. He just wanted to get home.

Jake left early, anxious to get beyond the growing town of Maley and head across a short stretch of flat land to the mountains. He'd debated the best route, and even though it was only April and the weather couldn't always be reliable, he opted to travel the mountains and follow the creeks and rivers rather than ride the flatter land north. Less chance of running into trouble in the mountains this time of year. He wanted to avoid more trouble at any cost. And Wild Bill walked out so well that he didn't think the mountains would present much of a problem. He'd still take a couple of shorter days, though, to get the animal into condition, just to be on the safe side.

He stopped in the former whistle-stop town of Maley in the late morning, soon to be renamed Willcox according to all the signs and banners hanging on buildings, and decided to eat a hot meal in a restaurant. It'd be his last good meal for many days. As he sat in the tiny café, he heard someone tentatively say his name. "Marshal Silver? Is that you?"

Jake looked up to see a short, round, bald man, hat in hand, standing two feet from the table. The man looked familiar, but Jake couldn't quite place him.

"It's me. Munsey. Munsey from San Simon. Our trails crossed in the mountains last fall, and you invited me to share your camp with you."

"Of course," Jake said. "I remember you. Sorry I didn't recognize you immediately."

"That's perfectly understandable, sir. It was dark when I arrived," Munsey said.

"How's the boy like his puppy?" Jake asked.

"The puppy and boy are doin' just fine…now," Munsey replied. "Course, that puppy ain't so little anymore."

When Jake saw the man wasn't thinking of leaving, he asked Munsey to join him.

"Why, thank you, Marshal. Don't mind if I do." Munsey pulled out a chair. "If you don't mind my sayin', you look like you've had a rough time."

"Indeed," Jake responded, not commenting more.

"I heard all about your troubles in the Chiricahuas, in Rucker Canyon," Munsey continued. "Glad to see you're doin' so well, all things considered."

The server brought Jake his meal, and he immediately began devouring the plate-sized steak and grits, hoping Munsey would move along. But that was not to be, and Munsey asked the waitress for a cup of coffee.

"Marshal, I was hopin' you were here lookin' for a certain man, the one everyone's now callin' the high country killer. Might that be the case?"

Jake raised an eyebrow at the news. "Haven't heard of him," Jake fibbed. "I've been laid up for several months." He purposely avoided asking about the killer and showed no interest in discussing the matter further.

"Marshal, I was hopin' you could help me out, and a bunch of others around here, too."

"I'm headed to Prescott now, Mr. Munsey. I won't be off looking for any varmints along the way. I've got important things to attend to in Prescott."

"I understand, but maybe you could just hear me out, and when your next choice of jobs come along, maybe you could pick this one?"

Jake sighed. He could see the man would discuss it one way or the other. "Mr. Munsey, I may not even be a lawman anymore by the time I get back. I don't want you to get your hopes up."

"That may be so, but I'd like you to hear me out anyhow."

Jake nodded. "High country killer, huh? Pretty fancy name."

"Yessir, it is. And it fits well. This man, Marshal, broke into my house sometime while I was gone, perhaps the very night I camped with you even, and had his way with my wife. She ain't never been the same. He scared her, and hurt her somethin' fierce. My boy, unfortunately witnessed it all."

"I'm sorry to hear that, Mr. Munsey. Truly sorry," Jake said.

"Well, that ain't all. We were the lucky ones. He went on and robbed, raped, and killed a passel of folks. One lone man. He shoots the men folk while they're out in the field working, or at least alone and without a weapon handy. Then he goes in and has his way with the women. Sometimes he stays at their house for a few days. Abuses 'em real bad. Mean man. He don't just shoot the men once either, Marshal. He rides up and shoots 'em point-blank range right in the face even after they're dead."

"How many so far?" Jake asked with growing interest.

"Six so far, I think. He ain't been around for awhile, though, but I heard tell there was similar trouble up in Snowflake a short while back. Like he's maybe movin' back that way again, headin' north. He started up there in that country."

"Mr. Munsey, I can't promise you anything, but I'll keep my eyes open. If I see trouble I'll do the best I can for you, but I can't go on a manhunt at this time."

"Well, Marshal, I 'preciate just anything you can do. That's the truth."

CANYON OF DEATH

"How's the boy doing?"

"Seems to be okay...mostly. But ya never know with these things. We'll be movin' on here soon, I 'spect. My ranch don't have much meaning to me anymore, what with my wife just sittin' and mopin' all day, every day, starin' at the wall." Munsey studied his coffee, avoiding the marshal's eye. In a low voice he said, "She don't talk. Barely eats. Won't let me get near her. Not sure what to do about it all, Marshal. I've prayed and prayed to the good Lord, but I don't get any answers."

"I'm sorry, Mr. Munsey. I wish I could help you right now, but I can't. I'm heading that way, though, so I'll keep my eyes and ears open. Maybe I'll run across this vermin. If I do, maybe I can take care of it." Jake said the latter, only to give the man some comfort. In truth, he hated the idea of having to deal with any more desperadoes at this point. He needed to get home.

Just to be on the safe side, Jake stopped at the gunsmith's and picked up more cartridges for his small arsenal. Then, lest he run into anyone else, he headed Wild Bill out of town, hoping to pick up at least ten miles before making camp. The days had grown longer, but because the nights were still right chilly, he had to plan on spending considerable time scrounging firewood. He knew he probably should have stayed in Maley for the night and started fresh in the morning, but he figured it wouldn't be long before Munsey would recruit more people to approach him for help.

Cold nights caused him to burn a brighter fire than he liked, and it quickly became apparent that Neil Erickson had been right – Jake's leg was in no condition to suffer on the cold, hard ground. Had he chosen another route, he could've stayed at way stations. As it sat now, he'd be out for possibly a good week, closer to two, before he'd get to any kind of civilization, and that only if the weather didn't turn colder yet and snow. Spring blizzards remained a possibility. He wouldn't be retracing his steps back to Snowflake or Kaibito, though. He'd be cutting West over the Mazatzals – a murderous range if there ever was one – then heading toward Prescott from there.

Still, he thought the trip remarkable, and after two days of seeing no traveler tracks of any kind, he began to relax and enjoy the beauty around him. Wild Bill found his rhythm, and the miles ticked off. For the first time in a long time, Jake allowed himself the luxury of self-reflection and reminiscing. At first, scrambled thoughts flitted in and out of his head, but eventually he decided to organize his thinking to make sense of things. He realized there was no point in going back and hashing out the difficulties that had arisen long ago between his father and him. He'd done that before. The old man had killed Jake's first sweetheart, a beautiful Cherokee girl, and he'd had her people butchered to keep Jake from running off with the young girl. His father had come back from the war a bitter, angry man who'd demanded his way in all things and who'd not spent an iota of time with Jake or his sister, Sophy. Only Jake's elder brothers had been invited to share in the old man's life. Ultimately he'd have to confront the old buzzard and get it all out in the open. Undoubtedly both of them would say regretful things. They'd certainly already said their share.

Instead, he focused on Betsy. He started at the beginning, the first time he saw her trying to buy a horse at the Mexican's place in Albuquerque. She and Thomas Jefferson had made quite a pair. Jake chuckled when he remembered the scrawny-looking kid and the black porter from the Atchison Topeka and Santa Fe railroad line bartering for the animal. Of course, Jake knew Jefferson from the train because the man had looked after Jake's horse while Jake rode as a passenger. But he'd never seen a boy quite like the one he encountered that day, and the kid had struck him as odd, but he'd ignored his gut feeling that something was awry with the youngster.

He'd seen the boy the next day also. Loading up to head out West, the kid had told him. Jake's instincts had urged him to take the kid into custody and look up his parents, but he'd let the incident go. The West was filled with boys looking to become men. Still, the kid's delicate hand and lack of experience had disturbed him.

Not for long, though. He'd come across the "lad" on the trail and had invited the youngster to travel with him for a bit. By that time Jake had become more than suspicious that this was one strange youngster. Nevertheless, he'd withheld judgment until he'd removed the boy's hat as the kid slept. That's when he discovered, not at all surprised by this time, the boy to be a girl. Quite a beautiful girl, at that.

Jake laughed aloud, remembering the girl's continued subterfuge the next day until he'd finally confronted her. She'd reluctantly admitted that she'd run away from the orphan train bringing her west to search for her mother and sister who'd been sent west two years earlier. The diminutive, petite lass claimed to be seventeen. Hard to tell. Still, he'd been both amused and chagrined by her situation and daring at trying to pass herself off as a boy in order to travel alone more safely. And he'd determined to make her accompany him to safety in Prescott. Once in Prescott, he'd delivered Betsy to Virginia Hall's boarding house, promising he'd go in search of Betsy's missing mother soon. He convinced himself he'd at last washed his hands of her, but each time he saw the girl, she'd continued to blossom into more and more of a beauty.

Called away to Freeman to rescue three kidnapped girls that locals had insisted were being taken by Indians, Jake discovered upon his return that Betsy had taken off to find her mother on her own. Infuriated with her and worried beyond reason, he'd left immediately in search of her.

Soon, after her rescue from robbers, the two became acknowledged sweethearts and talked of a wedding. She'd driven him wild with desire. Then she'd gone and inherited all that money from her mother's mining boyfriend, and things had turned sour for Jake. It galled him that he wouldn't be the man to support and care for her, that someone else's money had made her into an independent, extremely wealthy young woman. The trouble'd started when she'd suggested he stop being a marshal and become her houseman. Well, she hadn't said it exactly like that, but that's how Jake had felt.

He left her, only to return months later. He'd never stopped loving her, and he loved her passionately despite their differences now. There would never be another woman for him. Ever. He should have married her right off when he'd returned the first time, before he'd swept her into his arms and carried her into the bedroom. Why hadn't he? That was the question he had to answer before he could move forward. Why had he stalled? Now he'd created difficulties for the girl he loved by impregnating her. His child was illegitimate, and Betsy had become a woman with a reputation. It was his fault. But why had he not married her? Was it the money?

He suddenly realized mountain shadows were growing and darkness would soon be upon him. He looked for a likely camping spot and found one twenty minutes later, the same spot where he'd killed two gunmen who'd come in a group wanting to share his camp when he'd been en route south. Two had escaped, but he felt certain those two now lay dead in Chiricahuas in Rucker Canyon, Nantan Lupan's "canyon of death."

There remained no sign of the dead bodies he'd left for carrion months before. Either someone had come along and buried them, or they'd taken them to Snowflake for burial. Or animals might well have taken care of the two, scattering the remnants of the men's gnawed bones.

The next day Jake connected to a trail heading in a more northwesterly direction. He'd be traveling in what folks now called the Mazatzals, a ruthless area actively mined by a conglomeration of nationalities, including Mexicans and hostile Indians. He'd have to be more watchful, and he'd have to make sure Wild Bill remained securely by his side. The mule definitely would be a temptation for theft among this group.

He clearly understood what Ben McGraw had meant in Kaibito about the mule not being much for packing, but being a prize for riding. Jake had never ridden a consistently fast-walking, sure-footed, tireless animal. The mule was also much more alert and aware than a horse, although Jake didn't always appreciate the fact that the critter seemed to occasionally have a mind of his own. But, once he'd gotten over his disgust that he was riding a mule, a creature he'd never before fully appreciated, he could see that the animal had its advantages. "I owe you an apology, Bill," he said. "You're a helluva ride. Won't say anything bad about you again."

The rocky, steep trails in the Mazatzals made the going slower. Jake came across miners now and then, and all looked upon him with distrust and suspicion. He always stopped and spoke with them, hoping to elicit suggestions for shortcuts or easier trails. This was a territory Jake had heard a great deal about, but had little personal knowledge of. Few miners volunteered much information, nor did any invite him to stay and share their campsite for the night. The miners were, for the most part, a group of individualists who seldom worked together. It was each man for himself, although a few did form partnerships. Most partnerships seemed to end in the death of one of them, however, particularly after one of the partners discovered the precious metal they sought.

Jake no longer had the luxury to ponder his problems with Betsy. He had to pay close attention to the route and keep an eye out for Indians and

Mexicans. Both groups hated white men. Hell, up here, white men hated white men.

He still hadn't given thought to what he'd do if Betsy had married Gunner, something he couldn't believe, and didn't want to believe. He sighed. He hadn't come to any conclusion about why he hadn't married her, either. Why he'd procrastinated.

He'd think about it later.

WEDDING PREPARATIONS

The day following the news of Jake's survival, a tomblike silence hung over Betsy's household. To Tilly's dismay, Gunner absented himself entirely after he'd slammed out of the house the day before, and he'd not been seen since. Tilly'd gone to his quarters in the barn that evening, but Gunner hadn't been there. Tilly knew her son. She recognized that he'd want thinking time. Any man would, but at such a time as this, he might need guidance also, never having before experienced the ups and downs of love. She knew Gunner wouldn't want to hear her sage advice, which might have partly explained why he'd left. She would have advised her son to put the wedding on hold – perhaps indefinitely. She'd feared all along that Betsy would choose Jake over Gunner if Jake ever returned, and her intuition told her that Betsy cared for Gunner, but the girl did not love him like she loved Jake, nor would she ever grow to love him in such a way. Tilly thought it best to advise her husband of this turn of events. Like herself, he loved both Jake and Gunner. At this point Tilly wanted her husband's thoughts on the matter. Men viewed things differently from women. Maybe Ben would know the right thing to say to Gunner. She'd go into town and send a wire to Freeman. He'd get it soon enough.

***

Sophy sat at the table all morning, drinking coffee and entertaining Maggie. Despite her own experience with love and all its drama, Sophy could think of no advice to give Betsy. A part of her regretted having said a word about the letter, but she'd been so thrilled to hear from Peter and to hear her brother still lived, she'd not thought of Betsy or her impending betrothal.

CANYON OF DEATH

Another part of her had difficulty admitting that she'd shared the letter on purpose. She couldn't stand the thought of Gunner replacing her brother, whom she knew loved Betsy. Since she'd been living in the household, Sophy had been in constant turmoil with her feelings about her own life and engagement. Watching Betsy's relationship with Gunner progress, even by her own hand, troubled her.

In some ways, Betsy and Jake reminded her a bit of her former lover and herself. Their affair had the same zing of illicitness and adventure. But Sophy knew the love between Betsy and Jake was reciprocal, unlike her former beau, who'd been too self-centered to commit to Sophy in marriage. Sophy sighed. It would be a long day. An even longer two weeks until the wedding. Would Jake return in time to put a stop to it? After watching Betsy's reaction to the news that Jake lived, Sophy saw Betsy's upcoming nuptials as the biggest mistake of the girl's life. A mistake Betsy would rue to the day she died. A mistake that would cut Jake to the core.

She should move out of the household soon, she thought, particularly if Betsy married Gunner. It would be awkward to stay, being the former "almost-sister-in-law." She had some money. Perhaps she'd move to Virginia's boarding house until she and Peter wed. It would probably be best. Besides, she liked Virginia.

Suddenly, Sophy sat upright, her eyes widening in wonder. Virginia! She'd not told Virginia that Jake lived and was en route back. Virginia would surely know what to say to Betsy.

"Betsy," Sophy hollered from the bottom of the stairs. "I've got to run into town. It's quite urgent. Come get Maggie."

Betsy's bedroom door opened, and she slowly came down the stairs. Small dark patches under her eyes indicated she'd spent a sleepless night. She gave Sophy a small smile, then took the baby girl. "What's so urgent?" she asked, trying to sound casual it seemed, as though her whole world had not been turned topsy-turvy.

"I just have to run an errand very quickly. I'll be back as soon as possible. We should do a fitting of your dress today to see if we need to make any more alterations," Sophy said offhandedly as she put on a bonnet and riding jacket, testing to see Betsy's response.

"Yes. I suppose we should," Betsy answered in a flat voice, turning away. "Have you seen Gunner or Tilly?"

"I saw Tilly briefly this morning. I think she's taken the carriage into town. Haven't seen Gunner since…" she hesitated, "since yesterday."

When Betsy didn't respond, Sophy asked, "Will you be okay here by yourself, Betsy?"

"Of course. Don't be silly. I'll be fine."

***

Betsy burst into tears the moment the door closed behind Sophy. Maggie squinched her little face up in sympathy and also began crying. "We're a fine pair, Margaret Marie. Your mother has made a mess of things, hasn't she?"

"A mess? What's that mean exactly, Betsy?" Gunner stood in the hallway, a small bouquet of early spring flowers in hand. "If you're thinkin' of backin' out of this marriage, you best say so right now."

"Gunner!" Betsy said, flushing. "I didn't hear you come in."

"Came in through the back door."

"Have you had coffee or breakfast? Let me make you some," she said as she bustled past him.

"You haven't answered me, Betsy."

"Why would I change my mind, Gunner? I know I acted crazy when I heard Jake was alive. I was just relieved he wasn't dead. I wouldn't want him to die, even though I hate him and don't give a whit about him anymore. I was relieved for Sophy. And he *is* Maggie's father," Betsy said, walking quickly past him, avoiding looking at him.

"I figured I could be Maggie's father as well as he could," Gunner said, clearly unable to discern the truth of Betsy's explanation.

"Yes, of course. You'll be a terrific father, Gunner. Maggie loves you."

"Do you love me, Betsy?"

"Gunner! What a question to ask your fiancée!"

"You need to answer it then, if it's such a simple question."

"Gunner, what has gotten into you this morning? I declare you're not the same man you were yesterday." Betsy busied herself about the stove as she spoke.

CANYON OF DEATH

Suddenly Gunner grabbed her arm and spun her about. She tried to free herself, but she felt helpless against him. She'd always known Jake to be an invincible pillar of strength, but she'd never thought of Gunner as particularly strong or manly.

"I want an answer!" Gunner paused. "I need to hear it, damn it! I need to hear that you love me! Say it, Betsy! Say it or I'll…so help me…say it."

"You're frightening me, Gunner. I can't say I love you when you're threatening me like this. Let me go!"

Gunner reluctantly loosened his hold. "Can't marry you if you don't love me, Betsy. It's pretty simple." Both stood looking at each other for some moments, neither speaking. Gunner turned to leave when Betsy finally answered him.

"I do love you, Gunner. You've been so good to me. You've been wonderful and kind and helpful. I know I carried on yesterday when I heard Jake was still alive. But a tiny part of me still loves him, too. But you're the man I want to marry, Gunner. I want someone who's good, kind, and dependable. I'm sorry I carried on so. The news was just a shock. That's all. Just a shock. Jake means nothing to me now."

Betsy could tell by the doubt in his eyes that Gunner didn't quite believe her, or maybe he didn't trust her. "If you'd like, we can hold off on the marriage and wait until after Jake returns," she said.

Gunner slumped into a kitchen chair. "Why? So you can see which of us you like better? I won't play second fiddle to that bastard, Betsy. He let you down. Now he's wrecking our wedding," Gunner said, showing a dark anger Betsy had never before seen.

"Very well. To prove I love you, we'll get married on schedule. I was just suggesting this so's to reassure you that you'd still be my first choice."

"I'm thinkin' we should just go into town and see the Justice of the Peace and get it done with. Today. Right now." Gunner rose and walked toward her. "If you love me, Betsy, why wait?"

"I will marry you on the day we agreed upon, Gunner. I want to have a wedding. A real wedding. I want Virginia here. And Sophy. And Peter. And your parents. Don't take that from me!" Betsy began to cry, hoping tears would soften Gunner's resolve.

Gunner stood there, uncertain whether to pack up and move on, sweep Betsy off her feet and have his way with her, or do as she asked. "Christomighty!" he swore. "How long you gonna dangle me like this?"

"I'm not dangling." Betsy now realized she had gained the upper hand in this, their first argument. "You agreed to a wedding after Easter. You need to live up to your agreements, Gunner. Didn't you learn that?"

"Don't start in on me, Betsy," Gunner said, growing angry again. "You're the one who needs to live up to your agreements. You just remember that yourself. I'll be back. I gotta get outta here." He picked up his hat and stomped out the backdoor.

Betsy took a deep breath. She had to do some mighty serious thinking. If she'd wanted out of her upcoming wedding, she'd just had the perfect chance when Gunner had asked her if she wanted out, but she'd hesitated to cut him loose. From her sojourns into town, she was well aware that there were few men as good looking or as nice as Gunner. She shouldn't let him slip away. Whether she loved him or not was not important. What was important was that she be married for her daughter's sake, and for the benefit of the ranch, which was not an operation she could run alone. Gunner was her best choice. And in truth, she had grown fond of him with his dark, curly hair, chocolate-colored eyes, and winsome smile

But what about Jake? Jake would never be a ranch manager. He could be because he came from a ranching background, but he didn't like the work. She'd have to hire someone like Thomas Jefferson to run the place. Jake, however, was the handsomest man she'd ever laid eyes on. When he gave her that special look, she melted and could not refuse him. She loved him passionately and knew she always would. Sometimes she grew woozy just thinking of him.

Could she let Gunner into her bed? He'd never replace the man she really loved. That was the main problem, she realized. She loved Jake Silver with her whole heart, her whole mind, her whole soul. No matter what awful things he did, she loved him. She did not love Gunner. She was fond of him, but she could hardly bear to think of him touching her in that intimate way.

Nonetheless, as Jake always said, a man's gotta do what a man's gotta do, *and so does a woman*, she thought.

"I have two weeks. Two weeks to decide. I don't have to make a final decision today. If Jake shows up, then I'll cross that bridge. If he doesn't show up, the wedding goes on," she said aloud.

***

That evening, Betsy, Sophy, Gunner, and Tilly gathered for dinner, no one saying much, everyone taking their cue from Betsy, whose bearing was that of an imperial princess.

"Did you get your errand run today, Sophy?" Betsy asked.

"I did. And that reminds me, I ran into Virginia Hall. She said she'd like to pay a visit tomorrow. I told her that would be fine. I hope it is."

"I'm always happy to see Virgina," Betsy answered. "And so's Maggie."

"Tilly," Betsy continued, as though holding court, "I didn't see you all day today. Were you in town also?"

"Yes, dear," Tilly answered, offering no further explanation, resisting Betsy's royal demeanor.

When no further response came from Tilly, Betsy turned to Gunner. "Gunner, dear, what did you do today? I haven't seen you since morning."

Gunner looked up, shaking his head in exasperation. Finally, he answered, "Worked in the barn all day mending tack."

"Doesn't anyone want to know what I did all day?" Betsy asked after a moment's pause.

"Certainly," Sophy spoke. Tilly smiled, and Gunner looked up.

"I worked on my wedding gown. And I'm making a darling dress now for Margaret Marie. She will look the most beautiful of all of us, I'm sure. It's only ten days until the big day. But who's counting?" Betsy laughed.

"That's wonderful, dear. I should have been here to help you. I just thought…." Tilly trailed off.

"Please Mrs. McGraw – may I call you mother now?" Betsy asked, watching for Gunner's response.

"I'd be delighted for you to do so, Betsy."

"Well, Mother, Gunner and I had a talk this morning, and everything is going to be okay. As I told Gunner, I was just so shocked to hear Jake was alive. It's like seeing a ghost, really. Rather upsetting."

Tilly nodded, but Betsy suspected the older woman fully understood what was going on. Perhaps more so than even she herself did.

"Sophy, will Peter be back in time for the wedding? Did he say in his letter?"

"He said he wouldn't miss it for anything."

"I'm sure he wouldn't," Betsy replied, knowing full well that Peter's friendship included Jake only. Peter had made it more than clear on several occasions that he didn't particularly like Gunner.

"I've made Gunner's favorite dessert tonight, everyone. But let's retire to the drawing room, shall we, and I'll serve it there."

The three looked at each other as Betsy arose to dish up dessert. Although all knew that disaster loomed, no one spoke a word, each wondering when the storm would hit.

***

As Jake left the Mazatzals he breathed a sigh of relief. The remainder of the trip would be quick and easy. As it was, he'd saved a good three days when an old-timer had advised him of an unmarked trail. Even traveled with him a ways on it. At this rate, Jake figured he might even arrive in Prescott ahead of schedule. He'd hoped to be back the first of May, but it now looked like he'd arrive right after Easter.

Out of imminent danger from attack by outlaws, Mexicans, and Indians, Jake resurrected his thoughts on marriage. The moment the subject arose, he knew the answer. It was the ranch. It wasn't Betsy's fault she'd inherited so much, so the money was not the primary deterrent, although he did find it troublesome that she'd never really need to depend on him, that he wouldn't be her provider. It was the ranch, which represented her dream home. Jake didn't want to be a rancher. But if he married Betsy and she kept the ranch, that would pretty much force him to be one.

A lawman's life suited him. That's what he wanted. That's who he was. Lawmen didn't always make the best spouses, he supposed. Gone a lot. *Shot at.* Plain *shot,* he snorted since he now had the bullet holes to attest to that fact. Not a particularly good career.

After their first discussion, Betsy had never again raised the issue of his being a lawman. So why was it such a thorn in his side? *Is it because I know*

CANYON OF DEATH

I should turn in the badge and take up ranching if I really want to marry her and make her happy? He suspected that was the answer in a nutshell.

If she'd have him as the lawman he was, there was really nothing stopping him from marrying her, except his own guilty conscience about not doing the reasonable thing, the right thing.

Maybe he wasn't the best man for her. It galled him deeply to think that Gunner might be. More than galled him, Jake wanted to kill the little snot-nosed bastard when he thought about the boy moving in on Betsy.

Not being one to let the chips fall where they may, he felt he had to have an answer, a solution, before he reached Prescott. "Well, Bill," he said to the mule, "it's like this. If she's married, I just ride on outta there before I kill the groom. If she's not married, I'd probably better do some fast talking. Most likely she's plenty upset with me."

Deep down, he didn't fear, or respect, Betsy's anger or hurt feelings. He should, maybe, but he'd had his way with her from the first, and to his way of thinking, he'd sweep her off her feet once again. Just had to get there.

He spent quite a while planning the speech he'd deliver to her, and churning up thoughts of holding her. She'd fall into his arms and passionate love-making would follow. Those thoughts drove him about crazy.

Not much he'd say in the speech, really. He got Johnny Geiger. He'd heard he had a daughter. He loved her. He was sorry he left her, but he had to do what he had to do. That about summed it up. Concise and to the point. He'd fancy it up a bit, he supposed. He'd bring her flowers also. Women loved flowers, he'd heard. Oh, he almost forgot. He'd ask her to marry him, even though he'd already asked her at the Kaibito Trading Post. He'd ask again, anyway. Feeling confident, he whistled a tune, and Wild Bill's ears flapped back and forth in cadence.

"Maybe Gunner will take you back to Kaibito when I send that young man packing," Jake said after a spell. "Hate to lose you, Bill, but I'm bettin' your owner'd like you back. Maybe I can buy you." He resumed whistling.

Though the nights continued to be quite cold, the days grew warmer and wildflowers carpeted the hillsides. Yellow bitterbrush stood out the most, but the magnificent pink blossoms on the prickly pear caught his eye, too. Jake's favorite, though, was the silly-looking, spindly ocotillo, waving its skinny arms with tiny orange blossoms atop. Soon, the route would be heavily timbered, and the only cactus hardy enough to stand the higher altitudes would be the prickly pear, and even it didn't grow much at the mile-high altitude of Prescott.

The only thing that dogged him was that he had no plan if Betsy had already married. He didn't want to think about that possibility, but he supposed there was a remote chance it had come to pass.

If she'd already married that snot-nosed Gunner, he didn't think he could remain in the area. He'd have to relocate. He didn't want to ever run into Betsy in town, and odds were that he would. But what about his daughter, Margaret Marie? He had a right to see his daughter, didn't he? How was that going to work? He shuddered at the impending complications. *Don't trouble trouble til trouble troubles you*, his grandma used to tell him. Wise words. No point in worrying about the unknown. Still, once the thought entered his head, he had a hard time ignoring the insidious question: *What if she had already married?*

RETURN

Jake turned up the lane to Betsy's ranch. Wildflowers of every variety lined the road leading in, and his eyes feasted on the brilliant array of colors sprinkled throughout the green fields. It would be a good homecoming, he thought. While unexpectedly somewhat cool at this altitude, the azure sky had never seemed more beautiful.

Although a bit nervous at what might await him, he rode steadily on, resolving to handle things, and himself, with utter control. He plumb refused to think of Betsy as married. Focusing on the ranch house far ahead, he enjoyed the ride up the long drive, appreciating the beauty of the ranch like never before. He could see some fence rails needed replacing – something that he'd never have seen if Thomas Jefferson were alive and tending to the place. Jake would fix them first thing.

As he approached, he saw no activity. He'd expected to see someone out and about on such a glorious day. Riding by the barn, he heard the clang of a farrier's tools and he stopped, puzzled. Thomas Jefferson had always shod the horses. Who would be doing it now? When a man walked out of the darkness of the eaves of the barn to see who the stranger was, however, Jake immediately recognized Ben McGraw from Kaibito.

"You old son of a gun. What'd you do? Come all the way over here to get your mule back?" Jake asked, dismounting and clasping Ben's hand firmly.

"Told ya that mule was a good ride," Ben responded, shaking Jake's hand and smiling broadly. "Good to see you. But I gotta say you ain't lookin' none too good."

"Yeah, well, I ran into a bit of trouble down in the Chiricahuas."

"So I hear tell."

CANYON OF DEATH

"News certainly travels faster than this mule of yours. Who'd you hear it from?" Jake asked.

"Your sister got a letter from Captain Burt. She spread the word all over town that you were alive and well and headin' home."

"Well, it was bad. Real bad. Didn't think I'd live to see another day, but here I am."

"Heard your Indian friend saved your neck – again."

"Fortunately for me," Jake said. "Say, anyone around today? It's pretty quiet."

"Tilly and Gunner gone into town for some last-minute things. Sophy and Virginia are in town gettin' flowers and all kinds of what-not." Ben paused. "I suppose you've heard?"

"I've heard some rumors."

Ben cleared his throat. "Let me just say this, Jake. I love you like a son. So does Tilly. Always will, no matter the outcome of things. You remember that."

"Has the marriage taken place yet?"

"No. Supposed to happen tomorrow. I need to be honest with ya, Jake," Ben said, looking him straight in the eye. "As much as I love Gunner and want him to be happy, this marriage won't be good for him. He ain't ever gonna be happy, and she ain't never gonna be happy with him. It'll turn bitter. Everybody sees it but Gunner," Ben said matter of factly. "She loves you. But you know how women can be. They get their minds made up about somethin' and it's pretty much final. If anybody can stop this weddin', Jake, it's you. You best go on up there now. Betsy's alone. It'll give you some good talkin' time. And you'd better have a silver tongue in your head today, Jake Silver."

"Appreciate it, Ben. I'll head on up to the house now."

"I'll take care of Wild Bill for ya. I'll put your gear in the tack room in the barn. You git on up there."

Jake walked as quickly as he could without limping. He didn't want Betsy to see him limp if she happened to look out and see him coming. His leg had improved greatly, but it still wasn't quite what it had been. He'd been working on it, though, and forcing himself to walk normally, and the stiffness was showing signs of easing.

All the way to the house he contemplated the best approach. Should he knock? Walk in like he still lived there? Sweep her into his arms? He ran a hand over the three-day stubble on his face. He'd last shaved and bathed at a way station a few days ago. He knew he didn't look, or smell, his best, but that had never bothered Betsy before, and at least he'd made it back before the wedding.

As he started up the porch he heard a slight gurgling sound, and then his eyes alighted on his daughter for the very first time. He stopped and watched the tiny tot scurry on hands and knees toward a flower pot of nasturtiums, grab a small fistful and stuff them in her mouth. Jake could see Betsy in every feature of the child's little face. Babbling happily, the infant reached for another handful of flowers when Jake scooped her up.

"Hello, Margaret Marie," Jake said, his eyes welling and his heart suddenly overflowing with a love he'd never before felt. "I'm your daddy. Sorry I'm late." He couldn't believe he'd helped create the tiny, beautiful little creature in his arms. He blinked back tears of joy and held the baby girl out from him. "What're you doing out here all by yourself, young lady? Let's go see where your mama is."

The baby girl shrieked in delight as Jake gently swooshed her through the air. She grabbed onto him tightly and babbled incoherently, her large blue eyes never leaving his grinning face.

He took two steps toward the screened door before he saw Betsy silently standing behind it, watching him. He stopped, suddenly uncertain what to say despite his hours of rehearsal. Both stood, looking at the other, a myriad of emotions and thoughts racing through their minds, spilling onto their expressions, yet neither spoke.

Finally Betsy opened the screen and Jake entered. "The latch is broken. She gets out if I don't keep a sharp eye on her."

"I'll fix it right now," Jake responded.

"It's okay. Gunner says he'll fix it."

"Maybe we should talk about this," Jake said, more firmly than he intended.

"There's nothing to talk about, Jake. I'm getting married tomorrow. It's too late for talk." Betsy took the toddler and laid her in a bassinette. Swiftly she turned, took a full swing, and firmly slapped Jake's face.

CANYON OF DEATH

He'd seen the swing coming from the start, but made no move to stop it.

"How dare you show up the day before my wedding day!" she cried. "How could you do this to me? I hate you! I hate you!" she screamed as she began pounding ineffectively on his chest. "I never want to see you again." After a few moments, she sank to her knees crying. Jake moved to close the door, not wanting McGraw to draw the wrong conclusions from the ruckus, then he roughly pulled Betsy up.

"You listen to me, Betsy. I'm only going to say this one time, so you listen real good." He pulled her close, his face only inches from hers. "I love you like I have never loved another person. You're all I've thought about for the past six months. You're all I thought about as I laid in that Chiricahua cabin trying to get well so I could get back to you. My only regret the moment that bullet hit my back and I thought I was going to die was that I'd never see you again. If I walk out of here today, Betsy, I'll never come back. So before you go tossing me out, you make damn sure that's what you want to do."

Startled, she wrapped her arms tightly about him and sobbed. Despite her effort to talk, she could not stop weeping long enough to get the words out, and she firmly clung to him.

Jake held her, kissing the top of her head, stroking her back, trying to sooth her.

Slowly, she began to calm. "Jake, I've been so worried about you. So angry with you. I've hated you, loved you, and cried myself to sleep most every night."

"I'm here. I'm always gonna be here." He knew he'd said those words before and they probably sounded hollow. "I'll always return to you," he added, amending his statement. "Always."

Suddenly her lips were on his and he held her tightly as they passionately kissed. "I need you so much, Jake," she whispered. "But I can't be with you. I'm marrying Gunner tomorrow." That said, she broke free and ran up the stairs, closing the bedroom door.

Jake paused a moment, stunned by her rejection. He heard the bedroom door lock click, and without further hesitation, he took the stairs two at a time. He heard her yell for him to stay out, but he lunged at the door. Giving it a mighty kick, the wood splintered and the heavy door flew open.

"You stay away from me, Jake Silver," Betsy cried out.

And then he was upon her, and after a moment of resistance, Betsy willingly and eagerly surrendered to him, burning with need and love, melting in his arms.

They spent the morning loving each other, sometimes passionately, sometimes languidly, but at all times keeping one another in sight, continuously touching, embracing, and kissing. Neither mentioned the pending nuptials.

Later, Betsy drew a bath for the two of them, and it seemed like before, except for the little bundle that now napped in Betsy's rumpled bed, and Jake's gunshot scars. He smiled happily when he noticed his clothes remained folded in the bureau drawers. Later, they moseyed arm in arm down to the pasture, carrying Maggie. Abruptly, Moonlight's head came up, and the horse raced toward Jake, whinnying.

"Be careful, Jake. Moonlight's gone wild. Gun…" Betsy stopped, then went on, "I've been advised to get rid of him because he's so dangerous."

Her midsentence change did not go unnoticed. "Looks pretty friendly to me," Jake said as the horse approached and began nuzzling him. "I think he's fine."

"Honestly, Jake, he's been out of control. Charging people, rearing, kicking, biting. I've been so sad about it."

"Maybe he just hasn't liked his caretaker. I'll have him ready for you in no time," Jake said, smiling at her.

Both heard a carriage approaching and looked toward the barn to see Gunner and Tilly alight.

"Oh, no," Betsy murmured. "This will be awful."

"I'll take care of things," Jake answered. "You be still."

"Jake, I've got to be the one to tell him."

"I don't think you need to say anything, Betsy. He already knows," Jake said, watching the young man gesticulating wildly at his father.

***

"Where'd the mule come from, pa?" Gunner asked as he and Tilly brought the carriage to a stop. "Sure looks a lot like Wild Bill."

"It is. I loaned him to Jake," Ben McGraw said, after a moment of hesitation. "Loaned it to him after you left to take Betsy to Freeman."

"What? You mean that bastard is here? He's got a lot of nerve," Gunner said, his face reddening in rage.

"He's up at the house – gettin' to know his daughter, I suppose," Ben answered nonchalantly while giving Tilly a brief, knowing look. Turning back to Gunner, he said, "Before you go stormin' up there, son, you listen a dang minute. That gal up there ain't for you, Gunner. Everybody knows it but you. And maybe you know it, too, I'm thinkin'."

Gunner turned on his heel and marched toward the house. Part way up he spied the two of them standing with the baby at the pasture gate. They stood too close, like a family would stand. Like a couple would stand. Like a man and woman stand who know each other in that special way. Gunner slowed slightly, taking in the scene, his mind a jumble. But when he saw Betsy's wild horse affectionately nuzzling Jake, one thought stood out from among the others: he'd kill Jake Silver and shoot the damn horse, too.

As he approached, one look at Betsy's face told him all he needed to know, but he refused to acknowledge the message.

"Betsy, you best go on to the house. I have a few words to say to this lowdown, no-account asswipe," Gunner said, spittle flying.

Betsy gasped. "Gunner, you have no right to speak like that."

"Sure he does, Betsy," Jake said, stepping forward. "Why don't you take the baby and go on up to the house and close the door. I'll be there in a bit...darlin'."

Gunner's anger flared even more. The man was just too cocky for his own good, Gunner decided. He figured Jake had coldly calculated how to get under his skin, and he'd succeeded.

Both men stood, staring each other down until they heard the front door close. "You only get one free one, Gunner. Take your best shot," Jake said. "I figure maybe you have that much coming, although I'm not sure stealing a man's girl when he's down is any reason for a free punch," Jake said coolly. "But I'm giving you the benefit of the doubt that you didn't know any better, being so young and all."

Angered even more by Jake's attitude, Gunner took the first swing, and Jake let him. Shocked that he'd delivered a hefty punch with no retaliation, Gunner went for another.

"Not so fast. The first one you deserved – maybe. You only get one," Jake said, straightening himself.

Before Gunner knew what hit him, Jake landed three quick, solid punches to his face, knocking him down. Jake faked with his left and swung with the right, hitting Gunner squarely beneath the eye. He swung with the left to the jaw, followed by an uppercut with the right which sent Gunner to the ground. "I don't want to mess you up, kid. You had enough?" Jake asked as Gunner rolled onto his hands and knees, sputtering and spitting blood.

"You got no right coming here, Jake. She's marryin' me tomorrow."

"I don't think so. I believe the wedding's been called off."

Gunner stood, a bit unsteadily, but took another swing at Jake who easily dodged the telegraphed blow. Jake reluctantly delivered a rock-hard punch to Gunner's midsection, knocking the breath out of him. "I grew up with older brothers, and I can keep this up all day, Gunner. Tell me when you've had enough."

This time Gunner knew enough to stay down. He gasped for air, muttering and cursing when able. "I love her. I wouldn't ever leave her. You're never gonna stick around, and you know it."

"She doesn't love you, Gunner."

"You don't know that!" Gunner yelled. "You don't know a damn thing about that girl in there and what her needs are."

"You're wrong there," Jake replied, a cruel smile on his face. "I know her quite well, and we spent the morning getting reacquainted."

Infuriated at the implication, Gunner slowly pulled himself to an upright position, spat on the ground near Jake's boot. "Draw, you bastard. I want you dead, and then I'm gonna shoot that damn horse behind ya."

"Gunner, you're angry. You've got a right to be angry. But you're making a big mistake here. Don't do it. Don't go for your gun and make me have to kill you."

"No wonder you got shot up so bad down yonder. You talk too much, Mr. Big Mouth," Gunner taunted as he backed away, preparing to draw.

CANYON OF DEATH

"Stop it! Stop it this minute!" Betsy screamed, running toward them. "Both of you! Stop right now!"

"Betsy, get back," Jake commanded, his eyes never leaving Gunner.

Down by the barn, Tilly and Ben heard Betsy yelling, and they came running, hollering, and waving their arms. Still, Jake's eyes never left Gunner's face despite the hubbub.

"Son, stop right where you are because this has gone too far. I'm telling you. I'm your father. This has gone far enough," Ben cried, wheezing for breath from the uphill run.

The tension broke, and Gunner looked down. Still, Jake remained prepared, and sure enough, Gunner went for his gun. Before he had fully cleared leather, Jake fired, aiming low and expertly shooting the weapon out of the young man's hand.

A moment of silence, and then it was over. All of it, and Gunner turned to Betsy. "Is this how you want it?" he asked, his face bloody and bruised.

"I'm sorry, Gunner. Truly sorry," Betsy said, wiping tears away.

Gunner nodded and then looked menacingly at Jake. "We're not finished, you and me. You can count on it. Don't ever forget it. I'll get you, you sorry bastard," and then he strode away, Tilly running after him.

After a few moments, Ben McGraw approached Jake. "Thank you, Jake, for not killing my boy."

"I didn't want to do that," Jake replied.

"I know that. Someday he will too. All the same, I think we'd best be leaving." Ben extended his hand. "You take care of yourself, Jake Silver. Take care of this girl of yours here, too."

Jake nodded, and the two men shook hands.

***

It spread like wildfire that Jake Silver had returned and ousted Gunner McGraw, and three days later Jake received a visit from a friend and colleague, Sheriff Owens, over from Apache County.

Instead of preparing coffee to serve her guest, Betsy excused herself and went upstairs while the two men talked in somber tones in the parlor. The man's presence upset her horribly. Jake had been back a mere three days and already she felt certain the sheriff had come to pester him about another dangerous manhunt. She'd almost lost Jake this last time, and she couldn't bear the thought of going through that again. She resolved that if he accepted the job, she'd tell him to leave, this time for the final time. It didn't matter that the last three days had been the happiest of her life, what with their being so intimate, doing ranch chores together, and her planning a wedding. She wanted only to marry Jake and live the rest of her days with him always by her side. There'd never be another man for her. He didn't need to be a paltry deputy marshal. She had plenty of money. He needed to be a rancher. Her rancher, and a father to Maggie and the new baby she might possibly be carrying.

Straining, her ear pressed to the floor, she could make out the men's voices, and once in a while she could clearly hear a word or two, but most of what they discussed remained garbled and muted.

Soon, she heard greetings and laughter, and realized that Sophy and Virginia had arrived from town and had joined the men downstairs.

"Sheriff Owens, how nice to see you again. I hope you're not talking Jake into taking on a new assignment," she heard Sophy say.

"Just catching up on things," the sheriff replied, avoiding a direct answer.

"You're going to stay around aren't you, Jake? You won't be leaving for awhile, right?" Sophy asked, looking for confirmation.

"Nope. I'm sure Jake will enjoy staying here in the Prescott vicinity," Sheriff Owens piped up. "At least for the time being," Owens said. "It'll be lots of paperwork and home for dinner every night, right, Jake?"

Jake nodded, knowing full well that wasn't the meat of what he and Owens had been discussing. He figured his friend just didn't want to have to deal with the womenfolk on the sensitive subjects of cattle wars, let alone murder and rape.

"Listen, Jake, I'm going to leave. You got a lot of catchin' up to do. Come see me as soon as you can. I'm hanging out here in Sheriff O'Neill's office in Prescott for a bit then heading back to Apache County next week." Owens stood and prepared to leave. "Say goodbye to your beautiful girl for me, will you?" He picked up his hat, nodded to Sophy and Virginia, and left.

"You heard the man. I'll be around for a bit," Jake said, looking at the devastation on Sophy's face. "We'll have plenty of time to talk. Plenty of time." Except he already felt about talked out. He didn't know how many more times he could say the same things in a different way.

"What's that mean, you'll be around for 'a bit'?" Betsy asked from the bottom of the staircase. "You just got home. Three days you've been here. You were gone six months. Are you telling me you're leaving again?" Her voice began to rise. "Jake, I need you here! You have responsibilities here, whether you like it or not!"

"I was going to talk with you about that tonight," Jake responded. "Later. I'm not leaving right away. Maybe won't leave for a long while, in fact," he added, trying to ease her into the possibility. "But Sheriff Owens told me he's heard I've still got my job, so I'll be returning to work. Everybody's pretty happy, I guess, about the shootout in the Chiricahuas. It seems I've got some commendations coming."

Both Sophy and Virginia clearly sensing the rising tension, excused themselves to the kitchen to make a pot of coffee.

"I'm thinking I need to hire us a ranch hand and get you some domestic help," Jake volunteered. "You've got your hands full. I've got a lot of back pay coming it seems. Plus, those six men killed in the Chiricahuas all had a price on their heads. That's how I'd like to spend the money." Jake went on, not pausing. "I know a couple in town who'd do right by you. The man's a hard worker and knowledgeable, and his wife is a good housekeeper and can help with meals and the baby. Sophy will be leaving, you know, when she gets married. So you might want to consider taking on extra help." He talked quickly, yet tried to sound nonchalant, hoping to get it all in before Betsy threw a tantrum, if she planned on doing so, anyway. "You can raise champion breeding horses and keep mighty busy. That's something you've been talking about doing."

Betsy did not respond for a minute. Then she said, "Jake Silver, if you ever walk out of this house to go on another manhunt, don't bother to come back. I can't take it!" She ended in a yell, and Jake figured her fury stemmed from trusting that he'd actually give up the law and stay with her.

Jake studied her dispassionately, then in a deadly serious voice said, "I told you before, Betsy, and I meant it. Don't give me any ultimatums you aren't willing to live with." It was the same deadly voice he'd used with her three days ago. A voice he'd never used with her until then.

"I just did, Jake Silver. And I *can* live with it. If you're entertaining thoughts of going again, don't come back. Just take that horse out there and get out, once and for all."

"I got a right to see my daughter," Jake said, rising menacingly. "So I'll be back when it suits me." He approached her and at the last second decided to try one last tactic. "Let's not have to go through this again and again," he implored. "Just marry me, Betsy. You know I love you. You've known from the beginning what I am, and what I do. Don't try to take that from me. I'll always come back to you." There. He'd given her the basic facts straight up. She couldn't possibly ask for more.

"You make it sound so simple. And for you maybe it is," Betsy whined. "For me it's hell every time you ride out of here. I can't go through that anymore, Jake. I want you around like a husband should be. But go on, if it's that important to you," she continued, her voice hardening. "If being a lawman and chasing down criminals is more important to you than I am, then so be it."

He shook his head in frustration. He started to say that nothing was more important to him than her, but stopped. He stood a moment, looking at her, looking through her. "There's just no winning with you, is there?"

"Why don't you ask Gunner? But I'd say not," Betsy retorted.

. "I'll be staying in town. I'll send for my things tomorrow."

Betsy stood stock still, her face registering shock at Jake's callous, tough response. Jake himself was surprised at her unexpected resolve, but half proud of her for it.

"Stay wherever you will. It's nothing to me," Betsy replied, her confidence beginning to flag.

"And I'll be seeing my daughter any time I well please," he added firmly, striding toward her. He stood close, towering over her. "And the next child you might now be carrying, too, for that matter. You can't get rid of me so easily, Betsy." He pulled her to him and kissed her passionately. Even as she made a feeble, halfhearted attempt to struggle free, her response to his kiss more than reassured him.

Jake walked down the porch steps, brooding over the unexpected turn of events. But, after the turmoil of the last several months and his successful homecoming, he now knew for a certainty that he was Betsy's man, and he had absolutely no doubt that she was his woman. She wouldn't stray again. "Don't you worry, I'll be back," he said aloud to no one but himself. "And you'll be waiting for me, too." He smiled in the darkness and whistled for Moonlight, who met him at the gate.

Be watching for the next Jere D. James Western Novel

HIGH COUNTRY KILLER

TROUBLE IN THE HIGH COUNTRY

Jake Silver looked out the hotel room window at the bustling street below. No doubt about it, Prescott had sure grown since he'd come to the area. The whole territory would burst if movers kept arriving in record numbers. It seemed towns sprang up overnight in the most unlikely places. He wondered if it might be time to move on. Jake had remained in Prescott only due to the laxity of his supervisor who either didn't mind, or didn't notice, his prolonged absences, although Jake felt certain that his arrest record reflected well on the man. Jake also worked extremely well with different law enforcement agencies who needed help that only a federal marshal with unlimited jurisdiction could supply. A lot of small town sheriffs liked to see Jake ride into town to eliminate criminal elements.

Betsy had kept him in Prescott also. And now most likely his daughter would keep him close.

He strapped on his gun belt and out of habit checked the chamber of both Colts. Never had he found a bullet missing, but the routine remained. It would only take one time for a chamber to be empty, and it could be the last time.

He set his Stetson and glanced in the bureau mirror. He cut a fine figure. At six foot, well muscled and athletic looking, Jake Silver wasn't what one might consider a *real* big man, for he didn't pack the pounds. But he reckoned he was big enough to look both formidable and dangerous.

"Stay as long as you like. I've got some business to take care of. I'll be back tonight," Jake said to the sumptuous brunette sitting on the edge of the bed. "You gonna be around?"

"I'm working tonight, sugar," the woman answered, "but I can get off early."

"I'll see you this evening then." Jake winked at her as he closed the door behind him.

He exited the hotel and stood on the boardwalk, surveying the lively activity parading before him with the practiced eye of a lawman. He studied horses and rifle scabbards. The way a man sat a horse told him a lot, and the kind of rifle a man carried and horse he rode often told him even more.

Despite the early morning hour, already rough, rowdy talk issued from one of the saloons a few doors down where horses stood crowded together, sloppily tied to the rail. If the raucous yelling started this early in the day, it meant afternoon trouble for certain. Jake enjoyed a little action. In fact, he might stop by on his way to the sheriff's office to take a good look-see at who he'd probably be arresting, or shooting, later in the day. Sometimes just the appearance of a lawman caused trouble to foment.

Jake casually strolled through the batwing doors of the Lucky Lady saloon, covertly scanning the room. He sidled up to the bar and ordered a cup of coffee. "I see you got a lot of business this morning," he said quietly to the barkeep.

"Glad to see you, Marshal. That Billy Bradshaw and his gang came in an hour ago and been belting whiskey ever since," Lars Andregg replied, pouring Silver a cup of the blackest coffee imaginable.

"What's the occasion?" Jake asked.

"Hard to say exactly, but I heard talk about someone buyin' up a lot of property."

"Where the hell would Billy Bradshaw come up with two spare coins to buy anything, unless he stole it?"

"Not sure. Ain't heard of any stagecoach or train robberies, but he and Colton Dodd been buyin' drinks and actin' like they come into money. I dunno," Lars said, shaking his head.

Jake debated the advisability of wandering over and busting up the little party, but since no one had committed a crime, that he knew of anyway, he hesitated to intrude in their celebrations lest he cause trouble to start.

"I'll be back to check on things. No one's broke the law...yet. You got backup around here this morning?"

Lars nodded to the far corner of the room where his brother-in-law nodded in return, a rifle lying on the table beside his cup.

Jake raised his eyebrow in response. "Looks like you have everything under control."

"For now," Lars said. "For now, Marshal."

Once outside, Jake stopped to check the brands on the gang's horses. He surmised that two brands might have been altered, but if so it'd been done a long time ago. He moseyed on down the street, avoiding talking with the shopkeepers from whom he bought supplies. Jake didn't want Betsy's name to come up, and it seemed everyone had a mind to ask about her every time they saw him. It'd been less than twenty-four hours since he'd walked out on her. Word would get around in due time, he felt certain.

Sheriff Owens, clearly surprised at seeing Jake so soon after calling on him only the afternoon before at Betsy's ranch, heartily shook hands with him.

"I didn't expect to see you so soon," the Owens said.

"I didn't expect to be here so soon," Jake answered, off-handedly.

"You sure you're ready to go back to work?"

"I'm good to go. In fact, the sooner I get out of town, the better for all concerned," Jake commented.

Owens raised an eyebrow at Jake's response, but only said, "Good! You're willing to travel, then? We can sure use your help." The sheriff leaned back in a swivel chair, worry crossing his face. "We got serious problems. You heard tell of the 'high country killer'? That's what folks are calling him. Did Buckey talk to you about this yet?"

"We didn't talk business last night," Jake said, "but I heard of this killer when I was in Maley."

"That town's been officially named Willcox now, by the way, after General Willcox himself," Owens interrupted. "But, go on."

"Just heard about a guy who kills off ranchers and then abuses the women," Jake said. "Pretty hardcore even for the territory here, involving women in that way. Unusual."

"That about sums it up. A lot of local sheriffs suspect the fellow, or fellows, is back in the high country here in the northern part of the territory. That's where the crime spree started. It surprised me when reports came in that he was murderin' and rapin' as far south as Willcox," the sheriff said. "I don't see much point in the mayhem he's causing. It's not like he's walking off with lots of money or valuables. Just seems to be a cold-blooded, abusive killer."

Jake nodded in understanding, wondering himself what drove a man to do such dastardly deeds. It didn't seem like the gain was worth the crime.

"Could this be a gang? More than one man?" Jake asked.

"It's possible. That's the problem, see, is the only eye witnesses are the womenfolk, and they don't see the killing, they just see a man riding up all friendly like. Next thing they know they're being abused."

"Well, I know it's not Johnny Geiger, at any rate, since I left him dead in the Chiricahua Mountains," Jake said. "Hurting women was his pastime."

"It'd be a big help for all of us, Jake, if you rode on over to the Mogollon Rim country. The latest victims are from that area. Ask around. See what you can find out," Owens said. "I just can't shake the notion that this high country killer is from that area. I'm thinking maybe he traveled a piece and committed crimes elsewhere just to throw the law off."

"What makes you think that?" Jake asked.

"Well, three of the murders all happened in small settlements in the Mogollon area in a one year period. Then the next crime scene was Globe. Then on down near Willcox – in the San Simon area. But he only did one in each of those areas."

"That's interesting, because I know the victim from San Simon. In fact, the man wasn't killed. Just his wife was badly abused. I didn't think about him not being killed when we talked in Maley - Willcox," Jake said, correcting himself. "I wasn't really paying all that much attention to his problems. I had other things on my mind."

Sheriff Owens rustled through a small stack of papers. "That would've been Munsey down San Simon way. That the man's name?"

"Yeah. He camped with me one night when I was en route down there. Nice man. Bought his kid a dog."

"Well, Munsey not being killed could be another indication that the criminal was just trying to muddy the waters by going that far south. The facts are pretty clear," Owens said. "Three murders happened in the Mogollon area. Then two crimes occurred elsewhere. Then last week another one took place on the rim again. I think the Mogollon Rim is the nexus of the problem."

"You think these murders and the cattle wars are connected?"

"Haven't given it any thought, Jake. I don't see a connection, though."

"I'll leave day after tomorrow," Jake said. "I need to get gear and take care of a few matters."

"What do you know about the Mogollon area?"

"Well, I've not spent much time there, but I've heard it's pretty much Mormon country. Some little towns forming, but unless something's changed, nothing's too official yet." Jake sat a moment trying to recall other details about the area. "Fort Apache is close to the area. And there's quite a bit of cattle. Heard about the conflict going on in your area between cattlemen and sheepmen. Not surprising. Sheep and cattle don't mix well."

"That's an understatement. The cattle wars are keeping me on the go," Owens said. "Anyway, you've pretty much summed it up as far as the folks in the area. Lucky for you it's a good time of year to head into that country. I hear from high sources that the governor himself is getting concerned about this killing spree, so I'm bettin' you can charge up a mountain of goods for the trip."

Jake stood and the two men shook hands. "You may have some trouble brewing at the Lucky Lady, by the way," Jake said. "You might tell Buckey if he comes in today. I'll stop by and check on it this evening."

"Good to know. I'll tell Sheriff O'Neill when he comes in," Owens said. "Incidentally, I hear Morgan Smith is going to be appointed deputy sheriff here. You weren't interested in that position were you, now that it looks like you'll be settling down?"

"Nope. Morgan's a good man. He's got a wife and kid and likes being home come suppertime."

"Looks like you're kind of in the same predicament," Owens commented.

Jake's knew his lack of response as he headed out the door would tell Owens what he wanted to know.

Standing on the boardwalk, Jake felt excitement for the upcoming trip start to grow. Towns had their benefits, but the call of the wilderness continuously tugged at him. The main benefit of being a U.S. Deputy

Marshal pretty much boiled down to the total freedom that came with the job. Trouble was, the wilderness was quickly disappearing. Used to be a man could ride for weeks and not see a sign of human life, except for maybe Indian camps here and there, but now it seemed a rare day without coming across someone. Little hamlets might spring up simply because a wagon broke down on that spot. It provided a good reason for other folks to stop and tarry. Soon someone would build a store and then that one room, squalid structure became the center of a new settlement. A few villages failed because of their location and lack of water, but many thrived, attracting other small businesses.

Mostly men traveled the rugged wilderness areas alone, women being in short supply, which made these crimes particularly unusual. Usually, men treated females with a sense of wonder when the gals appeared on the western front. Men would remove their hats and stare in awe at even the most unattractive of females, simply because they appeared a most rare and marvelous sight for women-starved eyes of cowboys, miners, and wanderers.

Jake had even disrupted a bride-selling event in one tiny, bump in the road town when a man had pulled up with a wagon full of women for sale. Some nice-looking girls had been among the would-be brides, but the idea of peddling human flesh turned Jake's stomach. The seller remonstrated loudly, but Jake arrested him and escorted the young women to Yuma. Not sure what to do with the ladies, the problem resolved itself within an hour of their arrival when every single gal had found a man willing to be a lawfully wedded husband.

When women came West, children arrived soon after. Schools got built. Then churches. These things weren't bad, but the West would soon end up like the East if it continued. Where could a man go to be free of all these trappings?

Jake looked forward to a new assignment, for the Mogollon Rim still remained fairly wild country. Even though on a deadly manhunt, he would relish the hunt, the scenery, sleeping under the stars, and being free and unaccountable. He knew the lifestyle he'd chosen couldn't last. Either a bullet would put an end to it, or civilization would rob him of his pleasures. But he would give it hell while he could.

He strolled over to the mercantile, formulating a list of goods he'd need. He'd ride the *grulla*, Moonlight. Fat on pasture grass, the horse could use some mileage. He'd also take a pack animal. Too bad he didn't have access to the mule McGraw had loaned him when he'd gone on the hunt for Johnny Geiger. The animal had made an impression on Jake all the way to the Chiricahuas and back. Mules were hard to come by, and expensive, too. A pack horse would have to do.

He'd pick up extra cartridges and shells, and he'd buy a new rifle since he had reward money coming for killing Geiger and his band of outlaws, all of whom had prices on their heads.

Should he see Betsy before he left town? Probably not a good idea after being told to get out less than twenty-four hours ago. Besides, Lolly expected him this evening. She'd wasted no time in pursuing him when he'd walked into the Lucky Lady Saloon with Buckey O'Neill the night before. He would thoroughly enjoy that wild ride again, and it would serve to distract him from his other concerns. A good, if misguided, attractive and shapely young woman, Lolly knew how to pleasure a man. He'd need plenty of pleasure before the manhunt began.

Take a look at one of our other exciting Western books!

A Way in the Wilderness

Paula L. Silici

Chapter 1

Nathan spurred his horse to the top of the rise and reined in. Beyond him, broiling in the orange flames of the setting sun, a train whistled and wheezed at the depot like a long, black tea kettle letting off steam. Beyond the depot, tracks skewered the cattle town right up the middle, stretching east as far as the eye could see across the empty prairie. But Nate wasn't interested in the train, even though he'd be doing business with the railroad superintendent in the morning. What he was interested in at the moment was the rough-and-tumble, sprawling poor excuse for a town itself, Dodge City, Kansas.

Some of the tiredness eased from his bones as he shifted in the saddle and surveyed the town's layout. If he squinted he could just make out the bawdy red-and-black sign at the farthest end of Trail Street pointing the way to Miss Hattie Beachum's Black Boots Inn. The town might be homely, wild, and lawless, but just beyond its dirty skirts lay the finest little cat house this side of the Mississippi River.

As trail boss, Nate had been driving 3,000 head of Longhorns up from southern Texas along the hot, dusty Western Trail for months now. Bone weary, lonesome, and discouraged by the extreme difficulties his outfit had endured during the drive, he was anxious for a few distractions—like a hot bath, a soft bed, and filling up his belly with a good, woman-cooked meal. Distractions that would allow him to forget, for a while, the responsibilities he'd left ten miles behind on the trail.

He looked forward to the coming night, and smiled faintly as pleasant thoughts of Rosalie swirled in his head. The rest of what he was lonesome for would be his, too, in just a matter of hours. With renewed energy, he spurred his horse to a gallop and headed down the slope into town.

§

"Nate Barris, is that you?" Miss Hattie gushed as she advanced toward him, arms outstretched. As Nate's eyes drank in the scant, black lace- and red-silk ensemble that revealed more of her voluptuous body than covered it, he thought he'd never seen a truer personification of the word "madam" than Miss Hattie Beachum.

Cocking a grin, he said, "It's me all right, Miss Hattie. How are you? It's been a long time." He took both her hands and held her firmly at arms' length, thwarting her attempt to crush him to her ample self.

Hattie's smile slipped a bit as he watched her swallow his subtle rebuff. She recovered quickly, though, and replied with a fair amount of cheer in that smooth, Southern drawl of hers, "Yes, it has. Too long." She squeezed his hands then dropped them, stepping back a pace. "But I always say that once a man visits my Inn, sooner or later he comes back for more. You've just proved me right. Welcome back, Nate."

Her cool, assessing eyes gave him a none-too-subtle onceover. He stood there, grin in place, allowing her to do it, and wondering just what it was her eyes were telling her. He was used to women sometimes looking at him in bold, appreciative ways, but he never could understand what it was about him that women seemed to find so appealing. He didn't see his own face as being anything but ordinary, or his body as anything more than what God had given most other men.

He widened his grin, chiding himself. It was Miss Hattie's *job* to look at him like she wanted to bed him on the spot. Those hungry-eyed looks simply came with the territory. He could be as ugly as a buffalo's butt, and she'd still be looking at him like he was the handsomest cowboy she'd ever seen.

But then again, she'd seemed genuinely happy to see him, had even wanted to hug him hello. Miss Hattie always could touch that blasted soft spot in him. But at the present moment he was dirty as sin and stank to high heaven of cattle, sweat, and trail dust. How any woman, harlot or otherwise, could find him appealing enough to hug him in this repugnant state was beyond him.

Clearing his throat, he looked beyond her shoulder at a bawdy painting of a naked woman on the wall, then dropped his gaze.

Hattie laughed. "Still bashful, I see. You never did appreciate the decorations around here. Well, never mind. Let's get down to business. What is it you'll be needin' tonight besides a bath, Mr. Barris? I doubt you came all this way just for a drink and chitchat."

Nate laughed then, too, his face coloring as he started to apologize. "I know I'm a mess, Miss Hattie. I've got about twenty pounds of trail dust on me and only a skunk wouldn't object to my smell. Which is why I wouldn't let you hug me hello. I meant no offense, ma'am."

Clearly touched by his gallantry, her hand rose to her throat where she fingered the band of black ribbon decorating her neck. "Why, thank you for that, Nate. No offense taken."

A small drinks table adorned one corner of the room, and after snatching her silk wrapper off the back of a chair and slipping it on, Miss Hattie poured them both a brandy. Handing Nate one of the snifters, she said, "Men like you don't come along in this world very often, let alone to godforsaken Dodge City, Kansas. Forgive me if I forgot myself before. I was pleased to see you again, is all. Politeness and decency from buffalo hunters and cattle drovers is somethin' we don't see too often. Gentlemen like yourself are rare as virgins around here."

He could believe that. He supposed rough, mean, and crude would just about describe most of Hattie's clientele. Dodge City had the reputation of being the wildest town in the west, full of wooly buffalo hunters and raw cattle drovers, outlaws and just plain rowdy, shiftless no-accounts. After lifting his glass and taking a generous swallow, he said, "No need to apologize." He took another swallow and grinned again. "Lordy, but this is mighty fine brandy. Haven't had anything this fine since San Antonio."

Miss Hattie nodded. "My private reserve. Only the best for friends. Well, what else can we do for you this evenin', Nate? We're here and anxious to please."

Nate finished his drink and handed back the snifter, regretting he didn't have more time to linger over liquor this good. "Well, first off, I'll need a hot bath and a shave. A good meal wouldn't be out of order, either, and then...." He hesitated. "Hattie, do you remember from last time what I'll be needing after that?"

Hattie set down the crystal. When she looked at him again, her smile was broad and warm. "It's my business to remember, Nate. Of course I do."

He waited while Miss Hattie crossed the room to a bell pull and yanked it twice. In moments, a huge Negro giant of a man dressed in fine gentleman's attire and wearing a derby hat entered the drawing room. He removed the derby, stood at attention, and waited silently for instructions. Someone else, whom Nate couldn't quite see, waited just beyond the door.

"Mose, Mr. Barris will be needin' Cabin Number Five this evenin'. Please see that a hot bath is prepared, and have a bottle of my special reserve brandy and a dinner menu waiting for him when he arrives at his quarters."

The big man nodded. "Yes, ma'am," he said, bowing slightly. "Will there be anythin' else?"

"Yes. Tell Meg I wish to see her immediately."

As if startled, the giant hesitated for the briefest of moments before bowing a second time, then turning to do her bidding.

As he left, a young, garishly painted woman dressed in nothing but her red-and-black undergarments and long black boots, which were the signature attire for "employees" of the Inn, entered the drawing room.

"This is Mr. Barris," Hattie explained to the girl. "Please show him to Cabin Number Five and then come straight back here." The girl gave her a baffled look and Hattie chuckled. "I'm sure Mr. Barris would no doubt appreciate your special talents, sugar, but you're to do nothin' more than show him to his cabin and return. Do you understand, dear?"

The girl nodded quickly, her eyes dropping to the toes of her black boots. Turning to Nate she said, "Please follow me, Mr. Barris."

He gave the madam an anxious look.

"Don't worry, Nate. I remember everything you instructed me to do the last time you visited us. Unusual requests are nothing new to us here at the Black Boots Inn." She expelled another little laugh and gently placed her hands on her hips. "You wouldn't believe some of the peculiar things men ask for around here. But never mind all that. I'm just sayin' you aren't so different, Nate. Come mornin' you won't be disappointed. I promise."

Satisfied, Nate nodded, reached into his vest pocket, and pulled out several gold coins. "As you'll also recall," he told her, "I like to pay up front. This should cover things adequately, I think. I'll expect the young lady's knock on my door just after dark." He handed her the money, adjusted his hat, and turned to go. "It was good seeing you again, Miss Hattie. Thanks."

The madam dropped the coins into the pocket of her wrapper and flashed him another brilliant smile. "It's always good seein' you, too. Get along to your cabin now, and leave the rest to me. Enjoy your stay, Nate."

Other Moonlight Mesa Titles

Western Titles:

Stoney Greywolf Bowers, *Reflections from the Wilderness*, Cowboy Poetry, 2009.

Jere D. James, *Saving Tom Black*, A Jake Silver Adventure, Book I, 2009

Jere D. James, *Apache,* A Jake Silver Adventure, Book II, 2010

Jere D. James, *Canyon of Death*, A Jake Silver Adventure Book III, 2011

Rusty Richards, *Casey Tibbs – Born to Ride*, Biography, 2010

J.R. Sanders, *The Littlest Wrangler*, Award-winning Young Reader Western Book, 2010

Paula L. Silici, *A Way in the Wilderness*, Western Romance, 2011

Other Titles:

R. L. Coffield, *The Ben Thomas Trilogy: Northern Escape, Northern Conspiracy (The Thomas Bay Murders)* and *Death in the Desert.* Award-winning Suspense, 2005, 2009, 2011

Becky Coffield, *Life Was A Cabaret: A Tale of Two Fools, A Boat, and a Big-A** Ocean,* Award-winning Humorous Memoir/Travel Adventure.

www.ingramcontent.com/pod-product-compliance
Ingram Content Group UK Ltd.
Pitfield, Milton Keynes, MK11 3LW, UK
UKHW021312180426
11947UKWH00015B/1178